PRESUM

PRESUMED DEAD

THE DEATH (AND LIFE) OF GEORGE HART

BY

J. HOLDER

YOUCAXTON
PUBLICATIONS

ISBN 978-1-914424-07-6
Published by YouCaxton Publications 2021
YCBN: 01

YouCaxton Publications
www.youcaxton.co.uk

For Romy and Thea

Contents

Part 1

1980

"Who on earth rings the doorbell at this hour on a Saturday morning?" Wally complained. It was not that early but he was still in bed not yet having had enough sleep to recover from a typical Friday night out, celebrating nothing special other than the end of another uninspiring week at work.

Wally's question was not directed at anyone in particular but it was enough to stir Flick lying next to him. "Well, are you going to answer it or just pretend you didn't hear it?" Flick enquired, unhappy that her beauty sleep had been interrupted by the ringing of the doorbell.

Standing in front of Wally as he opened the door stood a courier; after handing him an envelope the courier asked Wally to sign a piece of paper, which he duly did. Wally inspected the envelope in his hand to see who it was from; the only clue was on the back of the envelope where the name "Haine and Pollard" appeared and below it the word "Solicitors".

Wally had never heard of them and was not in the right frame of mind to open the letter, not least because, from previous experience, letters from solicitors usually consisted of demands to pay outstanding utility bills. The letter would have to wait - at that moment the only thing on Wally's mind was the comfort of his bed and Flick lying in it; she might be willing to satisfy his stirring libido but she had other ideas, the only thing on her mind being to complete her rudely interrupted beauty sleep.

Over a cup of coffee a couple of hours later, Wally plucked up enough courage to open the letter and see what problem might be lying in store. Wally's shaking hands clumsily ripped the back of the envelope to reveal a one page letter inside. Reading the letter slowly, he could not make much sense of it, unsure if the letter was genuine. Keeping his thoughts to himself prompted Flick to ask him if everything was alright.

Her question did not get a response. Instead, Wally chose to read the letter out to her.

"Dear Mr Mortimer,

We have been instructed by the executors of the late George Hart; one of the executors is Mr William Haine, who is a partner of this firm. The executors have informed us that you are the sole beneficiary of Mr Hart's estate.

In order that we can proceed with probate and for Mr Hart's estate to be passed on to you, we require you to provide us with proof of your identity. You are therefore requested to call Mr Haine's secretary to arrange a meeting with Mr Haine at a time convenient to you; she will advise you what form of identity you will be required to provide.

Yours sincerely,
Haine and Pollard"

It came as no surprise to Wally that Flick's first question was to ask who George Hart was.

"I'm not sure. I don't know anyone with that name. Hart was my mother's maiden name but, as far as I know, she did not have any relations called George".

"Well, if I was in your shoes, I'd think about asking your mother if she knew of any George Harts" offered Flick.

Wally was not convinced he should ask his mother if she knew a George Hart in case the whole thing was a hoax or some other scheme to extract money from him. Before anything else, he would make enquiries about Haine and Pollard. Finding his Yellow Pages directory where he expected it to be, on a shelf next to the telephone, he thumbed his way through the directory; the third name listed starting with an "H" under the heading "Solicitors" was Haine and Pollard.

"At least they exist", he told Flick. He realised though that there was little point trying to call them as it was Saturday; the call to Mr Haine's secretary would have to wait until Monday at the earliest.

Being a son whose visits to his parents were less regular than they would have liked, Wally decided to invite himself and Flick for lunch the following day, knowing in all likelihood his parents would not have made other arrangements. If he was going to raise the subject of George Hart with his mother, he would rather do so face-to-face and over Sunday lunch would be as good a time as any. Wally phoned his mother who confirmed that she and his father had nothing else on the following day and they would love it if Wally and Felicia could spare the time to join them for lunch – it was only Wally's parents who took exception to calling Flick by something other than her real name.

Wally and Flick set off to his parents' home soon after 10 o'clock on the Sunday morning, allowing plenty of time to have an aperitif before a lunch which Wally knew would be served punctually at 1:00 p.m.

Wally's parents, Brian and Jill Mortimer, lived in a farmhouse two miles from the centre of Chipping Norton. They had moved there from Bristol when Wally was twelve years old having decided country life would benefit their only child more than city life – in reality, Wally was their excuse for a move that appealed to them more than to Wally. The move to the country meant that they would be closer to, but not too close to, the public school in Oxfordshire they hoped he would get into a year later, one that his mother was convinced would suit Wally better than his father's old school where the teachers still seemed to turn a blind eye to bullying and the demeaning initiation ceremonies imposed upon the new boys. Being a doctor, Brian had little difficulty in finding a practice to join in Oxford so, at least as far as Brian and Jill were concerned, the benefits of such a move outweighed any downsides.

Wally's teenage years in the country were pleasant enough but he knew well before he left school that, once it was time for him to earn his own keep, life in a big city offering more in terms of job opportunities and a social life would be more appealing.

Wally had made up his mind that today would be the day he would broach the subject of George Hart with his mother if the opportunity arose; he knew he would have to ask her at some stage and that the longer he left it the more difficult it might become. As he got out of his car, his mother greeted him with her usual hug and kiss on the cheek and her usual "How is my darling boy; have you been looking after yourself properly?" even though Wally had just celebrated his thirtieth birthday and had been looking after himself for a good ten years. His father's greeting was more formal, a shake of his hand before his parents turned their attention to Flick and welcomed her. It had taken a while for his parents to warm to Flick, initially because, to them, no woman was ever going to be good enough for their only child; now that Wally and Flick had been living together for more than three years, his parents were more concerned about whether they were planning to marry but at least they had the good sense not to ask.

As Jill worked away in the kitchen keeping a close eye on the leg of lamb (Wally's favourite) and vegetables roasting in the oven with a glass of Mateus Rose not too far away, Brian was in the drawing room with Wally and Flick, sharing a very agreeable bottle of claret, a 1978 Chateau Belair. The best part of the bottle had been drunk by the time lunch was served and Brian needed no encouragement to draw the cork from a second bottle.

Over lunch Brian and Jill fired away the same questions they always asked; to both Wally and Flick, how's work and how's the flat? And to Flick, how's your family? In return, Wally asked his parents what they had been up to and, as with their questions, their answers were pretty much the same as always – Mum was still playing her tennis and bridge once a week although finding a four for tennis every week at her age was proving more difficult than finding a four for bridge and Dad's still working hard although not finding it too hard to find time to play golf at least once a week. Although he recognised that his parents had their own lives and it was for them to choose what they did with them, their answers always left Wally feeling that they lived a narrower existence than he believed would suit him when he reached their age.

As Jill sat down at the dining table after serving up treacle tart with clotted cream (two more of Wally's favourites), a lull in the conversation caused Wally to blurt out "Mum, do you know if we're related to anyone called George Hart?" He had the second bottle of claret to thank for giving him the courage to bring up the subject.

"Why d'you ask darling? Is it someone you have met at work or what?" was his mother's response.

He did not want to reveal why he wanted to know or the existence of the letter he had received the day before, so merely replied that he had come across someone with this name and, as it was the same surname as her maiden name, he was intrigued to find out if by chance they were related.

After Jill said she could not think of anyone, Brian wondered if he could help jog her memory.

"Jill, I recollect your grandparents mentioning your father having had a brother but he was killed in the First World War and, from what I can remember, the brother was called George."

"Thank you, Brian. Now you mention it, I do recall my father having had a brother and I think he was called George but, as you say, he died over sixty years ago in the War. I don't recall though my parents ever talking about him. Maybe my father never wanted to talk about it."

Brian suggested to Wally that he could always ask Granny, Jill's mother, if she knew a George Hart but as she was now in a home suffering from dementia, there were no guarantees she would be able to recall whether she had ever had a brother-in-law or, even if she could recall having had a brother-in-law, what his name was.

Much as he felt better for making the trip to see his parents, it had not helped Wally as far as the letter was concerned. The only George Hart his mother could think of had died sixty years ago and there was nothing more he could do but wait and see whether Mr Haine could cast more light on the matter.

It was during his lunch hour on the Monday when he first tried to speak to Mr Haine's secretary but she too was on her lunch break, so not there to take his call. Wally left his name and number with the switchboard operator and asked that a message be left with the secretary to call him back. The secretary returned his call that afternoon and, after comparing diaries, arranged for Wally to meet Mr Haine at 11 o'clock in three days' time; Wally was told to bring with him either his passport or some other form of document by which he could be identified.

On the Thursday morning, Wally caught the tube to Chancery Lane in good time to arrive at the offices of Haine and Pollard in Lincoln's Inn Fields for his meeting. On arrival, he was ushered into a meeting room overlooking the Fields; it was not long before he was joined there by William Haine and a young lady whom Haine introduced as Clare, his trainee. Haine was not quite what Wally was expecting; instead of a man more his father's age wearing a pin-striped suit, with either thinning hair or a mop of grey hair, sitting opposite him was a man not yet forty years old who showed no signs of aging from the pressures of work. It was clear that Haine took pride in his appearance and it was not difficult to see why working in an office where the partners were not from her parents' generation would be more appealing to Clare; for a moment Wally wondered if the relationship between the two of them might be more than just a professional one.

After introducing himself and Clare, Haine asked Wally if he had brought in some form of identity; after he produced his passport, Haine asked Clare to take a copy of it for their file. Whilst she was at the photocopier, Haine took the opportunity to explain to Wally a bit about his law firm, which he and his partner Peter Pollard had set up some fifteen months ago. Although he did not tell any of this to Wally, they had both been working at another well-known firm of solicitors for over ten years but had become increasingly frustrated that the promises of promotion made to them continued to be broken; the reasons for this were obvious to Haine and Pollard – their bosses were more interested in lining their own pockets for as long as they could rather than sharing the spoils with the likes of William Haine and Peter Pollard despite the fact that they were the ones generating most of the spoils.

Haine did however tell Wally that he and Pollard were confident that, with the change of government the previous year, Britain was about to embark upon a number of years of growth and with that would come wealth creation for individuals to an extent not seen in Britain for many years. Haine and Pollard had set up their own firm so that they could be in a position to take advantage of this for their own benefit rather than for those who were less willing to put in the hours and less forward-thinking.

Wally was tempted to ask what all this had to do with the estate of a man he did not know but chose not to, preferring instead to hear what else Haine had to say for himself.

When Clare returned, Haine explained that he was one of the executors of the estate of George Hart who had died earlier that year and, as an executor, he was responsible for dealing with the wishes of Mr Hart, as set out in his will. Holding up the will, Haine continued speaking.

"Mr Mortimer, this is Mr Hart's will. It is full of what I call "lawyer-speak". Rather than read out it in full, are you happy for me to summarise it for you?"

After Wally told him he did not need to read it all out, Haine explained that, under the terms of the will, George Hart had named Walter Mortimer as the sole beneficiary of his estate; this meant that, after Mr Hart's liabilities had been settled and inheritance tax paid, George Hart's remaining assets would belong to Wally. Before he could ask what sort of assets Haine was talking about, he was told that, at the time of his death, Mr Haine owned a chateau in Normandy in France with a value of 4,000,000 French Francs, which equated to approximately £400,000 and other assets in the form of cash, shareholdings and paintings with a current value of approximately £2,000,000; Haine added that although Mr Hart had a sizeable estate at the time of his death, it was likely that its value, after inheritance tax had been paid, would only be in the region of £1,400,000.

Wally was flabbergasted. What was Haine talking about? He did not seem to understand that "only in the region of £1,400,000" was money beyond Wally's wildest dreams; this was money he could not remotely envisage ever earning or owning or, but for Mr Hart, inheriting. How could he expect to earn or own so much money working in the accounts department of a venture capital firm, where most his time was spent checking financial reports or producing accounts? Wally said nothing, not knowing what to say.

Haine explained the process of transferring the assets which had belonged to Mr Hart, adding that he was optimistic that everything would be transferred across to Wally within the course of the next twelve months; to try and justify why he thought it would take so long, Haine pointed out that, as some of the assets were in France, the French authorities would have to be involved and therefore more time than normal would be required to wrap things up.

Wally could wait; if it took twenty years, he could wait. He was troubled though not by how much or by when but by who? His parents had not been of any help and there was little prospect his grandmother would prove any more helpful. What if it was all a big mistake? What if the name of the beneficiary George Hart had put in his will was the wrong name and instead he had meant to leave everything to someone else? What if there was someone else called Walter Mortimer and Haine had contacted the wrong one? Wally was smart enough to know that, if it was all a big mistake, it would catch up with him at some time or other and that, if this were the case, it was better to know now.

"Mr Haine, I know this may sound an unusual question but I'm not sure I know who George Hart is or, should I say, was; do you have any idea why he has left everything to me?"

Haine was expecting this question, because George Hart had told him to expect it. George Hart had also instructed him that he was only to answer it on condition that Wally first asked his grandmother about George Hart. Although he knew the answer to Wally's question, Haine also knew for professional reasons he could not say more than he had been instructed to say by his client, even if the client was dead.

Instead of answering the question, Haine replied "When Mr Hart instructed us to draw up his will, we needed to satisfy ourselves that he was of sound mind; of that, we were in no doubt. He therefore knew he was leaving his estate to you and we were satisfied that that is what he intended to do. He did not explain to us why you were his sole beneficiary but he did tell us that your grandmother, Olivia Hart, might be able to help you."

"But she is in a home and suffering from dementia; what if she is not able to help me?"

"All I can tell you is that, if you want to know why you have inherited Mr Hart's estate, you need to speak to Olivia Hart."

Feeling a bit agitated at this response, Wally kept pressing "And, if she is unable to help, will you explain to me why I've been left what to me is a small fortune from someone I don't even know?"

"As his solicitor, Mr Hart did tell me a bit about his life. If your grandmother is unable to help, I can pass on what I know to you and it may well be that you can piece enough of it together to work more out for yourself. If it is any comfort, the inheritance belongs to you regardless of whether or not you ever find out why. But I'm not in a position to pass on what I know about George Hart until you've spoken to your grandmother. I appreciate that this is all rather cloak and dagger stuff and I quite understand why you should want answers to your questions but I hope that you too appreciate that I am honour-bound to comply with my client's wishes, even if he's no longer around to know whether or not I choose to".

Wally knew he was not going to get any more out of Haine. And as Wally had chosen to draw to a close his questioning, Haine decided to draw the meeting to a close. "Mr Mortimer, we'll be in touch again when we're in a position to transfer Mr Hart's assets to you. Thank you for coming in to see us and, if your grandmother is unable to help you, feel free to contact us again."

After the meeting, Wally took an early lunch before returning to his office in Moorgate. He needed time to himself to gather his thoughts which were firing off in two different directions, one about the fortune he would be receiving before too long and the other about his unknown benefactor. He was sure the money would change his life but he could not be less sure how George Hart fitted into his life.

Such thoughts continued to distract him throughout the afternoon and by 5:30 that afternoon he was anxious to get home and discuss with Flick what to do next. Flick had been able to get away from the art gallery where she worked near Piccadilly in good time to be home before Wally. Although he was keen to talk to her about his meeting with Haine, he thought twice about telling her how much was involved – it was after all his money– but he would value her opinion on what to make of George Hart.

After getting a cold bottle of Carlsberg out of the fridge for himself and pouring a glass of Muscadet for Flick, he sat on the sofa with his feet on the coffee table. Wally was the first to talk.

"How was your day at work?"

After replying "Pretty good – I think we sold a couple of paintings today; how was yours?", Flick realised that she had not asked how the meeting with the solicitor had gone, so quickly added "How was the meeting at Haine and whatever they're called?"

Not wanting to jump straight to the meatiest bits of the meeting, Wally started by telling her about Haine.

"Haine was younger than I was expecting and accompanied by a very pretty assistant whose only contribution to the meeting seemed to be to take a copy of my passport; he looks like the sort who likes to be seen in the presence of pretty, younger ladies and I reckon that's the reason she was there because she didn't have anything to say for herself. Anyway, Haine told me that George Hart has left me some money but, for some reason, he won't tell him who Hart was. I'm convinced Haine knows more than he was letting on but was claiming that he couldn't pass it on for professional reasons; all Haine was prepared to tell me was that, if I want to know who George Hart was, I need to speak to my grandmother."

Much as she was interested to know how much money Wally had been told would be left to him, Flick knew that she must not appear too interested; she knew Wally well enough to know that, if he wanted her to know, he would have told her.

"What if your grandmother can't help?"

"That's exactly what I asked; all Haine would say is that I should contact him again if she can't."

"That sounds to me as if he does know more than he's letting on."

"I'm sure that's right but, until I've spoken to my grandmother, I won't get any more out of him. I could of course just accept my good fortune in being left some money and leave it at that but, if I want to find out more about good old George Hart, I have to try and find out if Granny knows anything about him."

"Why d'you think your granny will know anything about him?"

"I can't be certain she will but Haine wouldn't have suggested contacting her unless he thought she knows something."

"And what if George did know your grandmother? Where does that take you? Assuming George died at an old age, d'you know if he was the same age as your grandmother?"

"I was so taken back by what I heard that I never thought of asking Haine how old George was or what he died from. Perhaps I should call Haine and ask."

"It can't do any harm."

"I can't do it now so it will have to wait until the morning."

Although he had lived with her for the best part of three years, he was not sure whether he should tell Flick how much money was involved. It was only fair that she should know but, instead of telling her, he decided to play his own little game with her and see how long she would last before asking. She cracked during her third glass of wine.

"Well, are you going to tell me how much you're going to inherit?"

Still stringing her along, Wally replied "I'm not sure; there will be inheritance tax to pay and liabilities to settle and I suppose Haine didn't want me to raise my hopes too high."

"Didn't he tell you?"

"He did give me a figure but it is by no means certain and I may have to wait a year."

"Well, what was it? £1,000, £10,000, £50,000 or what?"

"What."

Mistaking his answer for a question, Flick repeated her question with a hint of irritation in her voice "Is it £1,000 or £10,000 or £50,000 or what?"

"I told you; it's what"

"What d'you mean it's "what"?"

"It's not £1,000, and it's not £10,000 and it's not £50,000 and as it is not any of them, it must be what."

Flick now knew Wally was deliberately winding her up. "Wally, don't be a pillock; tell me what it is."

"Why d'you want to know?"

Flick thought this might be an opportunity for her to even up the score a bit.

"I just need to know whether, after three years with you, it's worth investing any more of my time with you or whether I could get a better return on my time investing it with someone else."

Wally had no doubt at all that she would have no difficulty in finding another man if that was what she wanted but he also knew that, had she wanted to, he had given her enough reasons to have done so by now. Much as Wally wanted to believe it would not happen, he could never be certain that it wouldn't and, much as he did not want to admit it, Flick's comment touched a bit of a raw nerve with him.

"As I said, I don't know for sure but I can tell you it's more than £1,000, it's more than £10,000, it's more than £50,000 and there is also a chateau somewhere in France." He added that if she really wanted to know the amount he was more than willing to tell her, but he could not resist a final tease. "If I do tell you, how will I know you're not just after me for my money?"

Flick realised that this was a good time to draw the subject to an end.

"Of course I don't need to know. All I need to know is that you love me and what you need to know, if you don't already, is that, for richer or poorer, I love you as well."

The following morning Wally telephoned Haine's office and was put through to Clare as Haine was out and not expected back before the afternoon. Rather than hang up, Wally asked Clare if she could help with a question he had, wondering if she, like Haine, would play the professional card as an excuse for withholding information.

"I'm not sure if you can help me but I'm sure you'll recall from our meeting yesterday that William told me that I would need to speak to my grandmother about George Hart. The trouble is that, for all I know, I could have a number of relations called George Hart and my grandmother may not know which one I'm asking about. Can you narrow it down for me by telling me what age he was?"

Clare wanted to help but was not sure if she should without Haine's say-so. Hoping to get away with it, Clare said she did not know but Wally would not take this for an answer. There must be something on the file which gave a clue to his age and, even if there wasn't, Clare would be able to hazard a guess at his age.

"Clare, I'm not asking you to tell me exactly how old he was but, if you met him before he died, wouldn't you be able to guess how old you thought he was?"

"I didn't meet him and I don't recall seeing anything on the file stating his age."

At least Clare was telling the truth when she said that she had not met George Hart and, although she knew there was likely to be something on the file which would disclose his age, she did not recall seeing anything and she was not about to offer to look.

"Presumably William's secretary met him so can you please put me through to her?"

To avoid appearing to be any more unhelpful, Clare was more than happy to do so.

"Hello, Mr Haine's secretary speaking."

"Hello, my name is Wally Mortimer. I had a meeting with Clare and Mr Haine yesterday. I'm trying to find out some information about George Hart. Clare tells me that she never met him but that you did. All I want to know is what sort of age was he". Wally was confident he would get away with lying about Clare telling him the secretary had met Hart without her questioning it.

Haine's secretary was more accommodating than Clare. After commenting on what a gentleman Mr Hart was, she said she did not know exactly how old he was but she would have put him in his early eighties.

That meant that he would have been born just before the end of the last century and that would put him at a similar age to Wally's grandmother but it did not mean that his grandmother knew who George Hart was. Nor did it mean that, even if she had once known who George Hart was, she could still remember him. The only way for him to find out was to visit his grandmother in her care home.

On Saturday morning Wally called the Cotswold Home for the Elderly to enquire about visiting times. Against her will, Olivia Hart had been moved into the Home two years earlier by her daughter Jill when Jill decided that her mother was no longer able to cope with living on her own – the final straw had come when she had left the taps in her bath running, with the resultant overflow causing the ceiling above her dining room to collapse.

Two years later though, Olivia accepted that it had been the right thing to do, not least because she enjoyed the company of the other residents in the Home.

Wally was told that visitors could visit patients at the Home at any time between 9:00 in the morning and 6:00 in the evening, any day of the week. As he did not want to use up a day of his precious annual holiday entitlement to visit his grandmother, he would make the trip over a weekend. Nor did he not want to wait until the following weekend before finding out who George Hart might be so decided to go the following day.

Flick didn't know if Wally wanted her to join him for the visit. "D'you want me to come with you?"

"It's up to you. If you have something better to do, don't feel you have to join me but, if not, you're more than welcome."

As she did not have anything better to do Flick agreed she would accompany him the next day. They arrived at the Home shortly after 11 o'clock and were taken to the reception where they waited until a nurse arrived to escort them to Wally's grandmother. As he had not been to visit his grandmother for over three months he asked the nurse how she was coming along. The nurse warned him that, because she had been diagnosed with dementia, she was not going to improve and that it was just a question of how quickly her memory deteriorated. Wally knew from his mother's visits that she did not always recognise her visitors but her current condition was more a case of loss of short-term memory than long-term. So far as finding out about George, that at least offered some encouragement to Wally.

The nurse located Wally's grandmother in the Home's gardens, sitting alone on a bench; she looked contented in her own little world staring back across the lawn towards the Victorian house which had been converted into the care home.

The nurse interrupted Olivia's peace and told her she had some visitors. As her daughter had been to see her the day before, she was not expecting any more visitors this weekend but her face lit up when she heard she had some more. Looking up she saw a young man and a young lady standing there looking at her. Her failing eyesight made it impossible to recognise her visitors so she asked the nurse who had come to see her.

Before the nurse could reply, Wally butted in. "It's me granny, Wally and I've brought some flowers for you. Do you remember Flick? She's come to see you as well."

"Oh how lovely to see you both and what lovely flowers. Let me smell them."

After smelling them and thanking Wally for them, she had to ask him who he had brought with him, even though he had already told her only moments before.

"I've brought Flick with me. You remember her, don't you? She lives with me in London."

"Is she your girlfriend?"

"Yes granny."

Olivia then invited them both to join her on the bench and tell her their news.

It was not long before Wally realised that his grandmother's concentration was not what it used to be so he kept his and Flick's news to a minimum. He made no mention of George Hart and instead brought the conversation round to Olivia and what she was up to. Olivia talked about her routine in the Home which consisted mostly of rest, reading, a spot of television in the evenings and listening to the radio. She had made a number of new friends at the Home but every once in a while there would be one less as old age got the better of them.

"Any new boyfriend, granny?" Wally enquired cheekily.

"Don't be silly; they're all far too old for me. I need a much younger man to keep me on my toes."

This light-hearted response made Wally feel this was a good moment to ask his grandmother about George.

Knowing there were only so many ways he could broach the subject, he did not want to sound too serious but this did still not stop him sounding a bit anxious.

"Granny, I've been meaning to ask you this for a while and I think you are the only person who will know. As you know, Mum has no brothers or sisters and I'm an only child, so I don't have many relations on your side of the family. I know very little about my family history and, as you're the oldest relation I have, I want to find out about it before it is too late. The thing is that recently someone mentioned to me someone called George Hart who is about your age. It didn't mean anything to Mum until Dad said he thought that grandpa had had a brother called George who had died in the First World War. Does the name mean anything to you?"

Olivia looked away. Wally could not tell from her reaction whether or not the name meant anything to her.

It took Olivia the best part of two minutes to gather her thoughts. Eventually she replied. "Did your mother say she thought grandpa had a brother called George who died in the War?"

"Yes granny but only after she was prompted by my father."

"Did she say any more?"

"No granny."

It seemed an age before Olivia spoke again.

"Wally, I will tell you about George Hart. There's not much point in me taking secrets to my grave, is there? What I'm going to tell you is not something your mother knows and I shall leave it to you to decide for yourself if you want to tell her. You should bear in mind though that it may be best your mother does not know."

Again she paused as if to gather her own thoughts before going on.

"Your mother was right. George Hart was killed in the War. What I have never told her is that George Hart was her father."

Wally did not need to be told that that made George Hart his grandfather but, if his real grandfather had died in the War, why had this been kept from his mother and why did granny think this was something his mother might not want to know?

Not wanting to confuse her, Wally chose not to tell his grandmother the George Hart he was enquiring about had only died a few months ago, so they could not be the same person. Instead, he chose to ask her more about her own parents and grandparents. With Olivia's long-term memory still lucid enough to recall her own childhood, she took great delight in passing on to Wally a lot more about his ancestry than he had known only an hour before.

Wally and Flick bade farewell to his grandmother before lunch and promised to visit her again soon. Rather than heading off straight back to London, they spent the rest of the day in the countryside; their first priority was to find a lovely country pub where they could sit outside and enjoy a typical pub lunch.

Over lunch, Flick waited for Wally to raise the subject matter of the bombshell his grandmother had dropped. She could not gauge how he had responded to the news that his grandfather was not who he thought he was and perhaps more how his mother would take it if she knew; it was clear enough though that it was something his grandmother had not wanted his mother to know and Flick could only presume that Wally's grandmother had her own good reasons for this.

Recognising that he was trying to take in what his grandmother had told him, she knew better than to engage him in conversation on any other subject so she kept her peace and waited for him to break the silence. After a couple of sips on his beer, Wally spoke.

"So what can we make of what granny said? Let's work it through. The first question to ask ourselves is whether or not granny is *compos mentis* enough to know if Mum's father was George Hart. If not, it doesn't take us any further and we're unlikely ever to get anything of any help from her. We'll then have no choice but to go back to Haine. But let's assume she still has all her marbles; was she telling us the truth? She certainly said it as if she believed it and is there any reason why she would tell us something if she didn't believe it to be true? We have to ask ourselves, even if she believed it was the truth, can we be sure it was the truth? Might she have imagined it? I guess we'll never know the answer to that either. So that leaves us with three scenarios; either she is away with the fairies too much to know the truth or she told us what she believed but it is not the truth or what she told us is the truth. Which do you think it is?"

Flick needed a bit of time to think which it was.

"Hearing her reminisce about her childhood makes me believe she knew full well what she was talking about, so I would discount the first scenario that she's away with the fairies. Was she telling us the truth? I can't say I know for sure but why would she tell us something which isn't? After all, if granny says George Hart is the father of your mother, we can safely assume there is no one better placed to know this. And looking at how much your mother looks like your grandmother, I think we can also safely assume that your grandmother and mother are mother and daughter. So, to answer your question, I think the most likely scenario is that George Hart is your mother's father. But, even if that is correct, where does it take us because the George Hart your grandmother knows died over 60 years ago and the George Hart who has left you a small fortune only died last year?"

Wally appreciated hearing her views; he knew he was sufficiently thrown by his grandmother's confession not to able to think straight and that, on his own, he might not be able to come to a rational explanation.

"I suppose one way we can find out if granny is telling the truth is to check if there is anything at the Register of Births and Deaths. We should be able to find a copy of Mum's birth certificate and that should state who her father and mother are. If George Hart is her father, we might also be able to find out when he died."

It was not until the following Wednesday that Wally found the time to visit St Catherine's House on the corner of Kingsway and Aldwych, where microfiche records of births, marriages and deaths were stored. He made his way to the reception desk where one of the receptionists asked him if she could help, in a voice which came across as if she actually did want to help. Wally explained that he was there to see if there was a copy of his mother's birth certificate.

The receptionist told him that should be possible and provided he knew when she was born and what her maiden name and given names were, it should not take too long. After providing this information – she had been born on 7th April 1918 and her full name before she married was Jill Margaret Hart – the receptionist asked Wally to take a seat. He did not have to wait more than ten minutes before the receptionist was able to show him on one of the microfiche readers a copy of his mother's birth certificate. Seeing the date 7th April 1918 under the column headed "Date and Place of Birth" and the names "Jill Margaret" under the column headed "Name (if any)", Wally was satisfied that this was indeed his mother's birth certificate.

He then looked at the column headed "Name and Surname and Dwelling-place of Father" and saw that the entry beneath this was blank. He did not know what name he expected to see but it came as a surprise to him to see there was nothing there. He asked the receptionist if she could explain why the entry was blank and was told that there was no legal requirement to include the father's name; she also informed Wally that more birth certificates than he might imagine did not include the father's name but she could not explain why the father's name had not been included in his mother's case. She also thought about telling him that many a birth certificate did include a name that was not the name of the real father but thought better of it.

After he had stared at the birth certificate for a couple of minutes, the receptionist asked if there was anything else she could help him with. Although the main purpose of his visit to St Catherine's House had been to find out if George Hart was his mother's father, he remembered that Flick had mentioned to him that, whilst he was at St Catherine's House, he might also be able to find out when George died.

"Presumably you also have copies of death certificates stored here as well. Would you be able to locate a copy of my grandfather's death certificate?"

"I should be able to if I have enough of the right information. Do you know when he died?"

"Sadly I don't. All I've been told is that he died in the War."

"Which war are we talking about? The First World War, the Second World War or some other war?"

"The First World War."

"Well, that narrows it down a bit. Any idea which year of the War?"

"Not really. I suppose it must have been some time after 7th April 1918 but I don't know."

"It'll take me a lot longer to find the death certificate if all I have is the year he died. Rather than wait now, why don't you come back in a day or two? I can't guarantee though that I'll have the answer. If he died in the War, have you thought about contacting the Commonwealth War Graves Commission as they might have a record of his death? Why don't you contact them? I can give you a telephone number to call."

"That would be kind of you. Thank you. I'll see if I have any luck with them."

After being handed the number to contact, Wally went back to his office. Slowly pieces of the jigsaw were coming together but there were still so many bits missing. Why had granny not wanted his mother to be told who her real father was? If his mother had seen a copy of her own birth certificate, surely she would have seen the blank entry and wanted to know why it was blank? If George Hart was his real grandfather, was granny's late husband, who Wally had always known as grandpa, really George's brother? Was it just a coincidence they had the same surname or were they cousins or related in some other way? Although some progress had been made, there were still so many unanswered questions.

That evening Wally recounted to Flick what he had learnt during his visit to St Catherine's House. It did not take her long to draw her own conclusions as to what he should do next.

"Wally, when we were having lunch on Sunday after visiting your granny, we discussed what the scenarios open to us were. One option is for you to tell your mother what you've been told; but I don't think your granny wants you to do that. If you tell her, it could cause her a lot of stress so I would discount your mother being your next point of contact. You could contact granny but what would that achieve? All you'd be telling her is what she told you could be true. That leaves contacting the Commonwealth War Graves Commission or Haine. Before you contact Haine, you should find out as much as you can and that means contacting the Commission."

Wally knew she was right and he felt comforted that she was able to work things out more objectively than he could.

The next day Wally called the Commonwealth War Graves Commission, only to be told that he needed to submit a written request for the information he was seeking. He was assured that, provided he included a stamped addressed envelope with his letter, he could expect an answer within seven days.

True to its word, the Commission responded to his request within seven days. The response came in the form of a printed document, not a letter.

HART, GEORGE

Rank: Second Lieutenant, Flight Commander

Date of Death: 29th November 1917

Age: 21

Regiment/Service: Royal Flying Corps

Panel Reference: Panel 2

Memorial: Cambrai Memorial to the Missing, Louverval

Other Information: Son of Albert and Alice Hart

This response revealed plenty of information that was new to Wally such as that his grandfather, assuming George Hart was his grandfather, had been a pilot in the War and was commemorated on a memorial in Cambrai, but the one piece of information that stood out was the date of death. George Hart had died five months or so before his mother was born. He realised that this did not mean George was not his mother's father, but merely that, if he was his mother's father, he had not lived to see his child.

Although this endorsed his view that his grandmother had been telling the truth about George Hart being his grandfather, it did not explain who George Hart, his generous benefactor, was. Had his grandfather not died in the War, he would have been of a similar age to the one who was Mr Haine's client but that did not count for much as Wally had been told by the only person who remembered him that he had died in the War.

Although piecing together the information he had gathered from his grandmother, from his trip to St Catherine's House and from the document he had received from the Commonwealth War Graves Commission had allowed him to conclude that his real grandfather might be George Hart, none of it helped solve the mystery of who George Hart the benefactor was. Feeling he had come to a dead end, he took up Haine's offer to contact him if his grandmother could not help.

Later that day, Wally called Mr Haine in his office. After telling Haine that his grandmother had not been able to explain to him who George Hart was, he asked whether Haine could provide any more clues or information about his late client.

Haine told him that, even if he had given the impression when they met before that he could help, the reality was that his client had never talked to Haine about his life and that, beyond the opinion he had formed about Hart from their one meeting, he knew less about him than he did his assets.

Haine was conscious that he was probably still coming across as being unhelpful, which was not something he was meaning to be; it did however prompt Wally to ask about George Hart's assets to see if they held the key to his life; if Hart had had the fortune that Wally was going to inherit, there must be someone who knew how he had accumulated it.

"When we met before, you mentioned that part of the estate was a chateau in France. Do you have any idea why he owned a chateau?"

"Yes, I do in fact. The chateau is in a village in Normandy and it is where Mr Hart was living when he died."

"How long had he lived there?"

"I'm not sure. I should be able to find out when he bought it but we did not have act for Mr Hart when he bought it. I can ask the French lawyer who is assisting us in passing title in the property to you."

"That would be hugely appreciated. How quickly will you be able to find out?"

"I can call them or I can send them a fax from this new facsimile machine we have just had installed, so it should be within the next couple of days."

The couple of days proved to be on the optimistic side and it was a week before Haine received a reply from his French counterpart, Henri Picault; Haine thought the delay was justified though when he realised that Picault had provided him not just with an answer to the length of time Hart had lived in the chateau but a history of the chateau itself. The chateau had been built in the first half of the sixteenth century and, in the second half of the seventeenth century, had belonged to King Louis XIV, who chose it as the home of one of his mistresses. In the Second World War, the Germans had taken it over and used it as one of their bases from which to administer the areas occupied by them in northern France. The chateau had been passed on to Hart and his wife when her father died in 1950.

The information Picault had provided was passed on by Haine to Wally and, although Wally recognised that the chateau he was going to inherit had an interesting history, what interested him most was the fact that Hart had lived there for the best part of thirty years.

Talking it over with Flick, he was convinced that there must be someone in the town or village nearest to the chateau who would know something about Hart.

"We're not getting much joy out of Haine and it seems as if this Monsieur Picault is one person we can speak to who may be able to tell us more about my benefactor; and even if he doesn't know much, he might at least be able to point us in the direction of someone who does know something. What do you think?"

"It can't do any harm, can it? Even if he isn't able to tell us any more, we won't be any worse off, will we?"

"How d'you feel about paying him a visit?"

"What? Go and see him in France?"

"Why not?"

Flick paused before answering.

"Because, if he can't tell us anything, it'll be rather a waste of time."

"No, it won't. We can go and look at my chateau."

"It's not yours yet but I have to say, it does sound rather a good idea. Can I come with you?"

"I'll have to think about that."

It was Wally's turn to pause before telling her that of course she could come.

After thanking him, Flick asked him when he was planning to go.

"I shall obviously have to check when Monsieur Picault is around and we'll both have to clear it with work. I don't suppose we'll both be able to get time off work for a few weeks as everyone seems to be away at present. It seems like it will have to wait until September which will probably suit Picault - if he's like every other Frenchman, he'll be taking the whole of August off anyway."

Wally and Flick agreed that they would try and see when in September they could take time off and Wally agreed to contact Picault to see when they could meet him.

When Wally contacted him over the phone, Picault did indeed confirm that he would be away for the whole of August and they therefore arranged to meet on Monday 8th September, allowing Picault enough time to catch up on any backlog of work that might have piled up whilst on holiday. With the summer holidays over and children back at school, neither Wally nor Flick had any difficulty getting time off work for their trip to France.

Picault's office was in Caen, twenty-five kilometres to the east of the chateau owned by the late George Hart. Wally and Flick arrived at the office at 10 o'clock in the morning on 8th September. Five minutes after arriving at Picault's office they were greeted by a casually dressed man in his early forties, his black hair slicked back and held firmly in place by whatever oil he used for that purpose; the tan gave away the fact that he had probably spent most of August working on it. Whereas Wally had expected Haine to have been much older than he was, in the case of Picault, his appearance came as no surprise.

He introduced himself to Wally and then to Flick, his lingering look in her direction leaving Wally in no doubt that Picault approved of her appearance.

"Monsieur Mortimer, it is a pleasure to meet you and of course your fiancée. Rather than sit in one of our rather stuffy rooms, please may I invite you to join me for a coffee in a delightful patisserie just around the corner."

Neither Wally nor Flick had any idea where Picault got the idea that they were engaged; Flick did not have a ring on her left hand but maybe it was no more than that Picault's English was not fluent enough to know the word girlfriend or maybe he just thought the word "girlfriend" sounded a bit common. Or, alternatively thought Wally, Picault had some ulterior motive and was trying to establish how committed Flick was to Wally. Either way, neither of them chose to correct him about their relationship.

Over the double expresso he ordered for himself and the *café au laits* he ordered for Wally and Flick, Picault spoke about the chateau's history, adding little to what he had already told Haine and what Haine had passed on to Wally. After the history lesson, Wally was keen to know what Picault could tell him about George

Hart and, when asked, Picault replied "I never had the good fortune to meet the man. He moved into the chateau not long after I was born."

Picault added "As I am sure you will understand, I did not represent him when he acquired it."

Recognising this as an attempt at humour, albeit French humour, Wally found himself grinning, as if to humour Picault in return, even if it was no more than a statement of the obvious.

"However, he was well-known to many people in this part of France."

"Would it be possible for you to arrange for us to meet anyone who knew him?"

"There are a number of people I could suggest. There is the housekeeper at the chateau – she has been kept on following Monsieur Hart's death at the request of Monsieur Haine to ensure the property is properly looked after. I think she has been the live-in housekeeper for a number of years so she may be able to help."

"Would it be possible for us to meet her at the chateau?"

"That should be possible. I should warn you though that I doubt she speaks a word of English so maybe you would like me to join you."

Although Picault's English was good enough, Wally was confident his French was better so he informed Picault that would not be necessary.

Keen to meet the housekeeper, Wally asked Picault if he would mind contacting her to warn her that Wally and Flick wanted to pay a visit to the chateau and to know when it would be convenient for them to meet her.

Later that day, Picault telephoned Wally at the hotel in Caen where he and Flick were staying and confirmed that Madame Dupont would be able to see them at the chateau on Wednesday morning at 10 o'clock. That gave them the next day to themselves.

They spent the Tuesday in much the same way most tourists to that part of France do. For their first sightseeing trip of the day, they walked from their hotel to the Abbaye aux Hommes to see where William the Conqueror was buried, after which Flick insisted they also visited the Abbaye aux Dames to see where Matilda, William's queen, was buried. They decided to have lunch at nearby Arromanches and then work off their lunch walking along the beach, trying as best they could to imagine the scenes there thirty-six years earlier, on D-Day when British troops were landing. They admitted to each other that they could not comprehend what it must have been like and their reflective mood meant neither of them felt they would fully appreciate taking in what they had planned for their final trip of the day, a visit to the Bayeux Tapestry; that would have to wait for another day.

By the time Wally and Flick set off on Wednesday morning to meet Madame Dupont, their sombre mood from the day before had passed and they had no difficulty finding their way to the chateau. It was located on the edge of the village of Montfiquet in grounds adjoining the royal forest Cerisy-la-Foret. The lawns each side of the driveway leading up to the front of the chateau had only recently been cut and whoever looked after the grounds clearly took great pride in their appearance. Although the chateau could not be described as grand, it was clearly as far as Wally and Flick were concerned a substantial property and one located in a most picturesque setting.

As they approached the front door, Madame Dupont opened it and greeted them. She eyed up Wally's features as if she was looking for something and, although there was something familiar about his looks, she kept whatever she saw to herself.

"Monsieur, welcome to what we hope will be a happy home for you. Please may I show you round the house. If you would like, I can arrange for Monsieur Dunard, who looks after the garden, to show you around outside after I have taken you on a guided tour inside."

"Madame, it is a pleasure to meet you. I would welcome a tour of the house; that would be most kind of you."

During the tour of the house, Madame Dupont informed Wally and Flick that she had worked as the housekeeper for over twenty years and although she did not say so, it was clear to Wally that she wanted to continue in that role. With Madame Dupont never short of a word or two as she took them through every room, the tour took a good hour to complete.

When it was over, the three of them retreated to the large kitchen where Madame Dupont offered them a coffee, which was most welcome, not least as Wally believed conversation over coffee might offer him the best opportunity to find out more about George Hart.

After thanking Madame Dupont for taking the time to show them round the house, Wally mentioned that it had come as a bit of a surprise to him that he had been left the chateau by George Hart without explaining why but that he was very much looking forward to spending time there. He also reassured Madame Dupont that he hoped that she would be willing to continue working there as housekeeper, appreciating that it would also make life much easier for him if and when he did spend time there. Madame Dupont looked most relieved to receive this assurance.

Flick could sense that Wally did not want to explain to Madame Dupont the principal reason for his visit and, as a consequence, he was unsure how to turn the conversation to George Hart so she decided to come to his rescue.

"Madame, I never had the pleasure of meeting Monsieur Hart so, other than what Wally has told me, I know little about him. If you can spare a few moments, I would really appreciate it if you could tell us a bit about what you knew about him and how he came to live here."

"Madamemoiselle, I can only tell you what I know and, as I only worked here for Monsieur Hart for the last twenty years or so, I can only tell you what I know about him for the past twenty years."

Madame Dupont took a sip from her cup of coffee before continuing.

"I started working here following the death of my predecessor. Monsieur Hart was living here alone and he needed someone to continue looking after the house for him."

"You say he was living here alone in this huge house?"

"Yes, he was. From what I have been told, he lived here with his wife but she died a few years before I started working for him."

"Do you know anything about his family?"

"No, other than that he had been widowed. Maybe Monsieur Dunard knows a bit more than me as he has worked here longer than I have. You should ask him."

"Thank you."

Dunard was all of sixty years old and managing the chateau's gardens had already taken its toll on a man of his age; the break from sweeping up leaves to show Wally and Flick around the gardens was most welcome.

The grounds were not too extensive and much as Dunard might have been able to cope with them in the past, Wally knew this was not likely to last much longer. As with Madame Dupont though, he did not want to leave Dunard with the impression that his days working at the chateau were numbered or that Wally would be seeking to replace him.

During the tour of the gardens Wally complimented Dunard on their condition and asked him how long he had been working at the chateau.

"My father worked on the gardens here before me. I started working here not long after Monsieur Hart acquired the property."

"Do you know who owned the property before?"

"It was owned by Monsieur Hart's father-in-law before the War but the Nazis occupied it during the War. After the War, the property was neglected until Monsieur and Madame Hart moved in following the death of Madame Hart's father." Dunard seemed tempted to spit in disgust at the mention of the Nazis but perhaps thought better of it in front of his new employer.

"Do you know where Monsieur Hart lived before then?"

"I'm not sure exactly where but I imagine it cannot have been far away because his wife was from this area."

"What do you know about his wife?"

"I knew who she was, everyone knew who she was. I cannot say though that I knew her well as we came from different backgrounds. Our paths did not cross."

"Why do you say everyone knew who she was?"

"Because of her family, which has lived in this region for generations and because she was beautiful."

"Madame Dupont told me Madame Hart died before Madame Dupont started working here."

"That is correct. I can't remember exactly when she died but I would say it was in 1958 or 1959, sometime around then."

"Do you know how long she had been married to Monsieur Hart before she died?"

"I know they were married before the last War but I don't know for how long. It should be relatively easy for you to find out though. The marriage will have been recorded at the nearest registrar's office and, if they were married near here, the records would be in Bayeux. If they also had a church marriage, there would be a record of it at the church where they married."

"I don't suppose you know whether they were married in a church?"

"I have little doubt that someone of Madame Hart's standing would have also had a church wedding. If I was you, I would ask at the church in Montfiquet."

"Do you know what Madame Hart's maiden name was?"

"Yes, Monsieur. She was Isabel Latour."

After lunch in one of the bars in the village square, Wally and Flick walked to the church nearby. The church was a typical Norman church and Wally guessed it was at least eight hundred years old. As the main entrance to the church was open, they went inside but there was no one there. The notice board close to the entrance gave the times of the services scheduled for the following Sunday but there were no other messages on the notice board to suggest when there would be anyone there to help them.

They made their way back to the bar to think through what they should do. They could not wait until Sunday to see the priest as they had to be back in London by then. Rather than pay the priest a call, they asked the bar's proprietor if anyone was likely to be looking in on the church before Sunday.

They were told bell-ringing sessions took place on Thursday evenings every other week and that the verger attended the church on Friday mornings to check everything was in order for Sunday's services. Friday would be their best bet.

Wally called the verger on the number he had been given and, after explaining why he was keen to see the church's marriage records, arranged to meet at the church at 11 o'clock on the Friday morning.

With Thursday to themselves, Wally and Flick went to see the Bayeux Tapestry. They knew from their schooldays a bit about the Tapestry, but seeing it for real exceeded their expectations, not least the scene they most wanted to see, the one depicting the arrow in King Harold's eye. They had thought about also using their time in Bayeux to inspect the marriage records at the registrar's office there but decided against it, confident they would find what they were looking for on their return visit to the church the following day; they could always visit the registrar's office on Friday afternoon if they drew a blank in the morning.

The verger was already at the church when they arrived there on the Friday and, after introducing himself, the verger took them into the vestibule where the church records were kept. The marriage records were in chronological order in several volumes recording marriages going back as far as 1792. Wally told the verger he did not know the year in which the marriage took place but, as the man whose marriage details he was looking for was, as far as he knew, in his early eighties, he guessed the marriage probably took place in the 1920s.

The verger passed the volume with the first entry dated 21st August 1919 to Wally; this volume contained the records of all the marriages that had taken place at Montfiquet church up until 1931. The verger left Wally to look through the selected volume telling him he would be not far away if he needed any assistance. Being a church in a relatively small community, there were not too many entries but progress was slow because the entries were in manuscript and, in many cases, the handwriting difficult to read. He was less than a quarter of the way through the volume when he came across the name he was looking for; there, under the heading "Bride's name" was the name Isabel Latour. Seeing the name caused Wally to gasp.

"I think I've found it", he uttered to Flick before even reading what else was recorded.

"What does it say?"

He read the rest of the entry to himself before informing Flick.

"It says Isabel Latour married George Hart on 10th September 1921."

"Is that all it says?"

"No. It says she was twenty-one and he was twenty-five years old when they married. It also records that he was born in London and that his parents were called Albert and Alice. Those are the names of the parents of the person I thought was my grandpa. This is just all too much of a coincidence."

"Can I see?" Flick asked, wanting to see the entries for herself as if not believing him. She saw for herself that everything he had told her was true.

Despite not believing it to be a coincidence, Wally could hardly believe what he had seen. The verger reappeared and saw that the two of them looking very confused.

"Is everything alright? Is there anything I can help you with?"

"No, that's very kind of you. I think we have seen all that we came here to see."

Wally thanked the verger again as he and Flick made their way out of the church. Doubting himself, he said to Flick "You did see for yourself what was in the register, didn't you? I wasn't making it up, was I? Do you think I should ask the verger if I can take a photograph of the entry?"

"You could ask but you don't need to as I have seen it as well and I know you're not making it up. I just can't work out what it all means."

Wally suggested that they find a restaurant nearby where they could enjoy a glass or two of wine and try and work out what it all meant because, at that moment, he was most confused by what he had seen.

Over lunch, they concluded that there were only three possible explanations. The first was that the person who Wally's grandmother told him was his grandfather and the person who married Isabel Latour were not the same person and it was just a coincidence, albeit an extraordinary one, that they had the same name and their parents had the same names; the second was that they were the same person; and the third was that the person who married Isabel Latour had stolen the identity of the person who Wally's grandmother had told him was his grandfather.

They discounted the coincidence theory. The chances of two men of a similar age having parents with the same names and of one of them leaving his inheritance to the grandson of the other was just too far-fetched and improbable for them to entertain this as even the remotest of possibilities.

They then considered whether the two George Harts were one and the same person. They were much the same age but, if they were the same person, how come Wally's grandmother and mother had both said that he had been killed in the War? If he hadn't been killed, what had made them think that he had been killed and why had the Commonwealth War Graves Commission recorded his death?

And lastly, they considered the identity theft theory. Although there was no evidence to support it, they wondered whether there might have been wartime situations where one person took the identity of another; they considered whether the man who married Isabel Latour had taken the identity of George Hart, knowing he had been killed, perhaps to avoid facing a charge for desertion or being absent without leave. If this had happened, why would Isabel Latour's husband have wanted to leave his estate to the grandson of the person whose identity he had taken? The only answers to this which they could come up with were either because Isabel's husband felt guilty about stealing another person's identity or because, over time, he convinced himself that he was the person whose identity he had taken.

Even though they had discounted the coincidence explanation, they felt that the other explanations were also highly unlikely but, of the two of them, the more likely, or the less unlikely of the two, was that George Hart had not actually died in the War.

Having decided that the two George Harts being the same person was the most likely of three highly improbable scenarios, they had to try and ascertain whether there was any information which might support such a speculative conclusion. The only way they could do so was to find out from Wally's grandmother why she believed George had died in the War; speaking to Wally's mother was not going to help because she did not seem to have any idea who he was, at least not until Wally's father reminded her that she might have had a deceased uncle called George. The next step was for them to return to the Cotswold Home for the Elderly and hope that granny's condition and memory had not deteriorated.

The weekend after they were back from their trip to Normandy Wally went to see his grandmother, this time without Flick. On his arrival at the Home, he was ushered into a large drawing room where his grandmother was sitting, gazing out of the window. It had been eleven weeks since his last visit and, remembering how her face had lit up when he presented her with flowers last time, he hoped that the flowers he had brought this time would have the same effect.

"Hello granny, it's lovely to see you again. I've brought some flowers for you."

The flowers had the desired effect and Wally's grandmother thanked him for being so kind. After chatting for a good thirty minutes about what she had been up to since he last saw her, Wally brought up the subject of George Hart.

"Granny, do you remember when I last visited you, I asked you about George Hart and you told me that he was my grandfather but that he had died in the War?"

"No Wally, I don't recall having that conversation with you."

Much as he was aware that his grandmother's illness affected her memory, such an answer was not encouraging but before he could think of how to respond, his grandmother continued.

"But, yes, it is true, George Hart was your grandfather and he did die in the War."

Wally was anxious to find out what made her think George Hart had died in the War but, rather than suggest to her that she might have got this wrong, he asked her what she believed had happened to George.

"As you can imagine granny, when you mentioned this to me before, this came as a surprise to me and I've been thinking about it since. Do you know how he died?"

"He was in the Air Flying Corps but was shot down during the Battle of Cambrai."

"Granny, who told you this? Was it someone from the War Office or some other official who had the horrible task of informing families?"

"No, Wally, it wasn't either of them. You see your grandfather and I were not married although I'm sure we would have been had he come back from the War. So the news was given to his parents and they had to tell me."

"Do you remember what they told you?"

"It was a long time ago but even though it was, I can remember it as if it were only yesterday."

Not wanting to interrupt her, Wally sat in silence waiting whilst his grandmother reflected and gathered her thoughts. It was another five minutes before she spoke again.

"They just told me that they had received a letter from George's station commander telling them that George was missing in action, presumed dead. He had taken off one morning taking part in the Battle of Cambrai but he never returned and his aeroplane was last seen losing height over enemy territory with smoke pouring out of one of the engines. His body was never recovered. It was such a shock to all of us at the time but that was that. It took me a long time to get over it but life moves on and you can't spend all your time fretting about the past."

Wally came to the conclusion that his granny believed she was telling the truth and that there was nothing to be gained by asking her any more. He did not know, and he was not prepared to find out, how she would react if he told her that he believed there was a remote chance that his grandfather had survived the War.

He stayed with his grandmother a further twenty minutes before bidding her farewell.

That evening Wally reported to Flick on his visit to his grandmother.

"You know Flick, if my benefactor had never turned up, I'd not have any reason to doubt that George Hart was killed in the War. But, because no one saw him die and because his body was never recovered and because a George Hart died only weeks ago, it just makes you wonder if the first George didn't actually die in the War. What is puzzling me is why, if he didn't die in the War, no one seems to have known about it. Surely, if he had survived, he would have returned to his family and granny. Surely he would have returned to see his only child."

After going over the same ground for the best part of two hours, they concluded that the case of the second George Hart might remain a mystery for ever. Some questions remained unanswered; if Wally's grandfather had died in the War, who was the man who had left Wally his estate and, if Wally's grandfather had not died in the War, why had he abandoned his family and loved ones?

They did not know the answers to these questions and they had no one else to turn to for help. Maybe they just had to accept someone had taken George Hart's identity but that still left another unanswered question - why had he left his estate to

Wally? Or was the existence of two men of a similar age, with the same name and whose parents had the same names just an extraordinary coincidence? The uncertainty left them feeling frustrated but, as they could do nothing about it, they resigned themselves to having to live with it.

Towards the end of October, Wally received a message on his new answerphone asking him to contact William Haine. As the message was left on his home phone, Wally only picked up the message after getting home from work, so the call back to Haine had to wait until the following morning.

Haine had called Wally to let him know that George Hart's estate could now be passed to Wally and that he therefore needed to discuss with Wally the transfer of George's assets to Wally. The remaining cash could be transferred to an account in Wally's name and George's share portfolio transferred to Wally. Most of the other assets which were to pass to Wally were stored in the chateau in France, the title to which had now been transferred to Wally. Even though Wally knew all of this was going to be his, it was a surreal moment when he realised all these assets were now his. What would he do with so much cash in an account which had only ever rarely been in credit? What was he going to do with a substantial property in France which he had no plans to live in? Who would look after it? What were the other assets there which he now owned? What would he do with a share portfolio, never having owned a share in his life before?

With such wealth came responsibility to look after it and, in carrying out that responsibility, Wally needed time. After explaining the situation to his boss and asking for time off, he was permitted to take two months' unpaid leave after which his job would be kept open but, if he wanted more time off, his boss could not promise that the job would still be there when he returned.

He was not sure how to explain to his parents why he would be taking the time off but knew he would have to tell them something. He could not tell them who his real grandfather, his mother's real father, was; equally, were he to tell them about the fortune he had inherited without telling them how it had come to him, he did not want them to think it was because of anything immoral or unethical on his part.

In the end, he settled on a white lie and told his parents he was being sent to France to work on a matter which involved managing the finances of a client; what he omitted to tell them was he was the so-called client. Much as he hoped that Flick would be able to join him in France, he appreciated that she would not be able to take the time off work, but they agreed he would come home every other weekend and she would make the trip to France the weekends in between his trips home.

On the first Monday in November, Wally caught the ferry to Cherbourg from Portsmouth. He was relieved that the weather was calm, making the crossing uneventful. After clearing customs, he headed for the small hotel he had booked himself into in Saint-Lo, a town a little under ten miles from the chateau - even though the chateau was now his, he decided not to stay the first night there, to allow Madame Dupont more time to prepare it for him. The following morning, he took his time over breakfast as he savoured his fresh orange juice, croissant and coffee; although very different to his standard breakfast of cereal and toast with a cup of tea thrown in, it would not take him long to acclimatise to French breakfasts.

After breakfast, he strolled around Saint-Lo to see what it had to offer and was pleased to notice it was a thriving market town which would provide for most of his needs. After his leisurely stroll, he made his way to the chateau.

Once inside his chateau, Wally hardly knew where to start; after familiarising himself with the layout of the rooms, he prepared a floor plan and produced a list of the contents of each room. It took him the best part of the afternoon to prepare a floor plan that was accurate enough for him to remember which room was where and how to access them. Despite his experience as an accountant stock-taking, the listing of the contents of each room was going to be a laborious task so he ended his first day's work at the chateau after preparing the floor plan. The following morning he worked his way through the rooms on the first floor, which consisted of five bedrooms and three bathrooms. There was not much to list in any of these rooms other than George's bedroom. The bed was still made up ready to be slept in even though it was several months since anyone had done so. The wardrobes were still full of George's clothes which had been well looked after. Although Wally did not want to keep them, he was not sure what to do with them; none of them were what he would choose to wear but he was loath to just throw them out or burn them. Maybe Madame Dupont or the gardener Monsieur Dunard would appreciate having some of them but he did not know if Madame Dupont had a husband or family that they might suit. In the end, he asked her.

"Madame, I see there are plenty of clothes hanging in the wardrobes upstairs. I don't think I'll have any cause to keep them but wondered if they might be of interest to you or Monsieur Dunard. If not, I could see if they might of interest to anyone in the market at Saint-Lo." Madame Dupont was delighted to be offered the clothes but Wally was keen not to upset Monsieur Dunard by favouring Madame Dupont.

"I shall also have to ask Monsieur Dunard if he would like any of the clothes and, if he does, we shall have to come to an arrangement as to who has what."

Wally was relieved to see that, if she was disappointed to have to share the clothes with Monsieur Dunard, she did not show it.

"I'll speak to Monsieur Dunard to see if we can sort out a time when the two of you can agree what you want and I can then deal with whatever is left over. Perhaps it would be better if we do this when I have finished going through the rest of the house to see if there is anything else I won't want to keep."

Listing the contents of the downstairs rooms was going to take longer than the upstairs rooms but with another three days before the weekend when Flick would be joining him, he was in no hurry; he would complete the task by the end of the week and then ask for Flick's view as to what he should keep and what he should give or throw away.

The rooms on the ground floor consisted of a hall, a kitchen, a large drawing room, a dining room, a study and a second, smaller drawing room, along with a cloakroom and a separate toilet. In the hall were various paintings including some portraits hanging above some antique furniture, a grandfather clock and a worn out rug. Had the frames to the portraits not included brass nameplates, he would not have had any idea who they were but even knowing their names did not mean much to him; presumably they were of previous owners although he doubted any were of the mistress of Louis XIV who had lived there 350 years ago.

Working his way through the hall and the kitchen had taken up all morning and, wanting a break from the tedium, he took a light lunch in one of the bars in the village. He went for the busier of the two, assuming it was the busier because it was the better of the two; he would try the less busy one the following day.

Walking into the bar, Wally was conscious that a number of the locals turned to look at him. He found a table to himself and ordered a *croque monsieur* and a glass of the draught beer to wash it down with. The beer was served straightway and, by the time the *croque monsieur* was served, his beer was ready for a refill. The food was brought to him by a woman who he took to be the proprietor's wife; he visualised her working away in the kitchen whilst her husband stood behind the bar chatting away to the locals perched on stools by the counter; every once in a while, the chatter was interrupted as the husband attended to an order for drinks.

As the bill was presented to him, the woman he assumed to be the proprietor's wife enquired what had brought him to this neck of the woods. Wally noticed that, as this enquiry was put to him, the conversations elsewhere in the bar seemed to quieten down as if she was not the only one who wanted to hear his answer.

He was unsure what the reaction would be if he said he was the new owner of the chateau; would they resent a foreigner and one as young as Wally owning such a property? Instead, he replied that his mother was related to the late George Hart who had left the chateau to his family and he was there to ensure it remained habitable whilst no one was living there. This seemed to appease his audience, with the proprietor's wife telling him that any relation of George Hart was more than welcome in the village. Wally was relieved that his answer had been well received and that it had prompted such a warm-hearted response.

On returning to the chateau, Wally tackled the larger of the two drawing rooms. Hanging on the walls in the drawing room were paintings by artists unknown to Wally but artists who, if not the best known impressionists, painted in their style. Since going out with Flick, he had learnt enough about art to know that they had been painted between 1880 and 1910 and that they would fetch a very good price if he were to sell them. In the corner in the drawing room was a piano with two silver photo frames on top of it. In one of the frames was a black and white photograph of a bride and groom whom he reckoned must be George and Isabel; the other was of a woman lying on a beach looking a picture of happiness and as if she had not a care in the world; comparing the two photographs, he recognised the woman lying on the beach as the bride in the other photograph.

By the end of the week Wally had finished going through the rest of the downstairs rooms, leaving just the cellar and the attic to attend to. Of the downstairs rooms, only the study had been of any real interest to Wally because of the photographs there which he hoped would cast more light on George's life.

On Friday evening Flick took the overnight ferry to Cherbourg and Wally was there to meet her as she came through customs early the following morning. Wanting to spend the weekend at the chateau rather than at a hotel, he drove them straight to the chateau from Cherbourg, only stopping en route at a boulangerie to buy some freshly baked croissants.

After a leisurely breakfast at the chateau, they paid a visit to the market in nearby Saint-Lo, stocking up with food for the weekend and some additional provisions Flick thought were needed.

Over lunch back at the chateau, they shared a bottle of Muscadet as they tucked into their baguette, ham, saucisson, pate and brie, after which she had a rest, her lack of sleep on the overnight ferry catching up with her.

Whilst she was resting, Wally made his way down into the cellar to see what was down there and was delighted to see it had been put to good use, storing a not insignificant wine collection. Wally enjoyed his wine but could not claim to be an expert; he knew enough though to know from the names on a number of the wine boxes that there were some serious vintages stored there and he would take great pleasure not only in taking stock of the cellar's contents but also working his way through them. He needed time to check which ones were ready for drinking and which ones would continue to improve but that did not stop him selecting for consumption that evening a couple of bottles of 1975 St Emilion, knowing he would enjoy them now even if they were likely to improve over time.

The two of them did not know what to expect of their first night in the chateau. The surroundings were unfamiliar but they both enjoyed being together again in the comfort of a large double bed. Despite having rested earlier in the day, Flick had no trouble getting to sleep and, having had more than his fair share of the two bottles of wine that he had opened, nor did Wally.

The only thing on Wally's agenda the following day was to check out the attic, the only space in the house left for him to inspect. He did not know if there was anything there other than pipes and a water tank. Access was through a hatch in the ceiling above the landing at the top of the stairs attached to which was a ladder. He entered the attic tentatively, half expecting to find vermin living there - if there were any bats in the attic, he had not disturbed them, which he took to be a good sign. High enough for him to stand up, he walked slowly around the attic, keen to ensure he did not disturb anything untoward. There were signs that wasps liked to nest there but he knew there should not be any flying around this time of year. Clunking noises came from the pipes and at the far end of the attic he could see where the water tank was located.

Walking back to the hatch to make his exit, he noticed an old suitcase lying there. Wondering if it had been left there just to keep it out of harm's way, he nudged it with his foot. As it did not budge, he reckoned there was something inside. Rather than inspect its contents in the attic, he eased it down the ladder, opening it up on the landing at the top of the stairs where the light was better.

Seeing him struggling down the ladder with the suitcase, Flick came to his help.

"What've you got there?"

"It looks like an old suitcase. "

"Did you find anything else up there?"

"No, just the water tank, some pipes and a few wasp nests."

The suitcase contained various private papers and mementos. They were also some albums containing photographs taken over the years from the early 1920s to the early 1950s; as with the private papers, Wally would need time to digest what was in the albums and who the photographs were of.

Also in the suitcase was a leather-bound notebook with nothing on its cover to suggest what was on the inside. Turning the pages quickly, Wally could see that its contents were hand-written. The last page was dated June 1960. Turning back to the first page, Wally started reading it.

Seeing he was engrossed, Flick asked him what was in it.

"I can't tell from the first page that it'll provide us with the answer to the mystery about the two Georges but I think we're about to find out a lot about my benefactor."

"What makes you think that?"

"Let me read to you the first couple of paragraphs."

Wally then read out aloud the first page.

"The first half of this century has seen civilisation at its worst; two World Wars, brought about by greed, have caused unparalleled suffering. Both have transformed lives, some for the better but many for the worse.

I am one of the fortunate ones who survived and luck played a major part in my survival. I owe my life to the kindness of many people, both friend and foe. I also had my share of suffering.

It is my hope that future generations will never have to experience what my generation has been through and that historians will look back on this period in our history as a turning point. It is my hope that politicians throughout the world will also look back on this period and recognise that there are only losers in war.

It is also my hope that, in the future, historians and politicians will have access to undistorted records which allow them to have a clear understanding of the suffering endured in war; maybe the record of my own experiences will help them to have that understanding.

Only time will tell if my hopes are fulfilled or misplaced."

Wally stopped reading. He turned the page and saw that the second page started with the words "I was born in 1896".

"Flick, I think I'm about to find out a lot more about George Hart".

Part 2

1896-1917

George Hart was born on 26th June 1896 at his parents' home in Barnes, in south-west London, the first of Albert and Alice Hart's two children; his brother, Edward, was born on 15th January 1898.

Being less than nineteen months apart, the brothers were very close, despite the occasional squabble. Being the older of the two, George was, whilst they were growing up, the bigger of the two and Edward very much looked up to his older brother.

Their closeness suffered a setback when George was sent away to boarding school at thirteen but the setback only lasted two years until Edward joined him at the school. George had not settled easily in to his new school; the older boys were like men and most of them only too keen to treat the younger boys and, in particular, the new boys in the way they had been treated when they had started. This meant new boys putting up with somewhat random beating by the school prefects, all too often dished out for no good reason. George had no one to turn to for support when he was on the receiving end of such unjust treatment and just grinned and bore it in the same way as everyone else.

Having an older brother at the school meant that, when Edward started, he had someone to turn to for help, both physically and emotionally; the older boys were only too aware that brothers usually supported each other as if working as a team and the chances of any comeback for their bullying were greater if they picked on those with an older brother.

In his last year at school, George was made a school prefect but did not use this position as an excuse to punish the younger boys unfairly. Being a prefect was not a licence to treat younger boys the way he had been treated; in his view, it was for the masters to hand out punishments and then only when they were merited. The younger boys knew where they stood with George and, as a consequence, earned him their respect.

As a school prefect, George's chances of winning a place at Oxford University were enhanced and, recognising this was an opportunity not to be missed, George put in plenty of extra hours of work in his last year at school. His efforts were rewarded when he was offered a place at Christ Church College to read classics.

He accepted the offer without a second thought and left school at the end of the summer term in 1914. Little did he know on his last day at school how within the next three months the lives of so many people across Europe and elsewhere in the world were about to change.

George's extra hours of studying had not prevented him watching developments taking place across Europe, although no one was certain what would happen following the assassination of Archduke Franz Ferdinand during George's last week at school. There was much speculation in the press and how it might affect Britain but no one knew for sure. Even after the Austro-Hungarians declared war on Serbia on 28th July and the Germans declared war on Russia on 1st August it was not clear how it would affect Britain; but three days later the British people were in no doubt that they were not going to be left untouched by events on the Continent as war was declared on Germany. Many questioned the wisdom of Britain's decision to go to war as there was no immediate threat but the decision was made and the British people would have to live with it.

Having secured a place at Oxford to start less than two months after Britain had declared war, George sought his parents' advice on what he should do; should he volunteer or should he take up his place at university? His mother Alice did not want him to go to war for no better reason than that she did not want him to risk his life. George's father Albert was more prepared to consider and discuss the reasons for and against volunteering.

"George, you are under no obligation to fight for your country. But what if all your peer group volunteer and you're the only one left behind? People will take you to be unpatriotic and possibly cowardly."

"Father, not all my peer group are volunteering so that's not a reason for me to volunteer. Of course, were I to find that I was one of only a small number not fighting, I would reconsider my position."

"The newspapers are predicting that the War will be over within a matter of months. How would you feel if you missed out on all the action?"

"I don't believe what we're reading in the newspapers is realistic. I can understand they want to be positive and encourage people to fight for Britain but I don't think the German army can or will be defeated within a matter of weeks or indeed months. They've been preparing for war for much longer than we have and to suggest that we can overcome them in the short term is, I believe, fanciful optimism. We'd stand a better chance if we were fighting them on home soil but fighting them away from home in a foreign country will not be the same. The German race is not so different to us – even our King and the Kaiser are related; they'll fight as hard as we will so I don't see why anyone should think it'll all be over soon."

"George, you may be right and, if you are, there will be plenty of time for you to join up. You should think long and hard though about whether you should be prioritising a place at university over fighting for your country."

"Father, of course I shall and, in doing so, I'll take full account of your views and those of Mother."

The discussion with his parents had helped him in some ways but not in others. His mother had made her position clear but George was unclear what his father's view was; his father had raised issues which he should take into account in making his decision but had not expressed his own view what George should do. Maybe having one parent's view clear and the other not expressing a contrary view would make George's decision easier but what if his father was really of the view that he should volunteer? He would speak to his father again but only when he had given himself more time to think things through.

"Father, I've given a lot of thought since we last spoke about whether I should take up my place at university or whether I should volunteer. I've considered the points you made and also Mother's view on the subject. I don't want to do anything against your wishes and, much as I respect and understand Mother's view, I'm not clear what your view is or what your advice is. In a nutshell, do you think I should volunteer or do you think I should go to university?"

"George, I too have considered your views on the War and whether or not it will all be over soon. If I was in your shoes, I'd choose to go to university. If your views are right and you choose to go to university, there will be plenty of opportunity to join up later and fight for your country but if your views are wrong and the War is over quickly, you will miss out on fighting for your country."

"Father, I appreciate what you're saying but I'm not sure if you're saying you think I should choose to go to university; what you're saying is that you understand why I'd come to that view but not that that is your view."

"George, you are a perceptive boy. You have asked for my view but ultimately, it's your decision. I should not be making the decision for you. All I ask is that you are rational when coming to your decision. And, if you are, I'll be fully supportive of it."

George made up his mind to go to university just a month before he was due to start, much to the delight of his mother but, despite having made his decision, he was not immune from the pressures to volunteer. The posters of Lord Kitchener pointing his finger with the simple message that his country needed him were everywhere and he was often confronted in public by women who, because their loved ones had volunteered, wanted to shame George into signing on. What the posters and women did not tell him, or indeed anyone, was how the War was going; less than six weeks into the War, British troops had been engaged in two major battles and the casualty numbers were escalating; the six days of the Battle of the Marne in the first half of September had seen thirteen thousand British casualties and the four days of the First Battle of the Aisne in the middle of September even more. The newspapers were full of the Germans being forced to retreat but it did not count for much with the Allied forces being unable to break through the German trenches. Just six weeks into the War so many lives had already been lost and the Allied forces had only reclaimed something in the region of twenty kilometres of land taken by the Germans. It only confirmed to George his view that this war was not going to be over quickly.

His decision not to volunteer was further vindicated when word reached him that two of his contemporaries from school were amongst the casualties. Neither was a close friend but he remembered them well enough to know who they were; he wondered whether they had been lured into volunteering in the belief that the War was little more than a game which the Allied forces were bound to win. He was in no doubt though that, whatever the reasons, they did not justify the ends.

Although he was well aware that his decision to go to university at a time of national crisis was not, in many quarters, a popular one, he was determined to make the most of his time there; there might come a time before long when he would be required to sign up and, were that to happen, he did not want to go to war feeling that he had not made good enough use of his time at university, however brief.

George did not take long to settle in to life at university. How he spent his time was down to him rather than his tutors but with the extra freedom came responsibilities. No longer was he required to attend lessons but instead he decided for himself which ones to attend; no longer did he have to be in bed by a certain time or worry about being caught in a pub or smoking although he knew his parents would disapprove of the latter. Games were no longer obligatory and he could choose for himself which sports to take part in. Rowing could wait until the summer but, as a way of meeting people, George joined the college rugby team; after a trial, he played regularly for the college second XV, with the occasional promotion to the first XV to cover when there were injuries. The difference in standard and in the levels of fitness between the two teams was significant and George felt more comfortable when turning out for the second XV.

He was also keen to join the Oxford Union, not least because the programme of debates throughout his first term was so topical. The motion for the second Union meeting of the term, held in early November, was "This House supports compulsory conscription". Such a motion was bound to arouse interest amongst students who would be affected if compulsory conscription was in place and George was determined to be there to hear the debate. Arguments in favour and against the motion were put forward; those in favour argued that it was the duty of every fit and able man to fight for King and Country whereas those against argued either that there was no such duty to fight or that any duty to fight was limited to defending King and Country at home rather than in some foreign land. Those in favour argued that the government was bound by treaty to declare war following Germany's invasion of Belgium and Luxembourg whereas those against argued that young men should not be forced to fight against their will because of treaties passed in 1839 and 1867 by governments they did not elect and nor should they be forced to fight for their country on the back of a decision of a government they were too young to vote for. George did not speak during the debate but listened intently to the speakers. He cast his vote against the motion and was relieved to see that, with the motion not being passed, he was not in the minority.

After the debate, George retired to the Union bar and, just as he was about to order a drink for himself, a young lady came and stood right next to him. With such a well-attended debate, the bar was fuller than usual and as the young lady brushed against him, George looked at her. Half expecting her to apologise for bumping into him, he was taken back when all she offered was a hello. Having been brought up with no sisters and having only attended single-sex schools, he could not recall a woman ever greeting him in this way before; even his lectures at Oxford consisted mostly of men as there were only a handful of women reading classics. Instead of remonstrating with her, George said hello back before realising the gentlemanly thing to do was to ask her if he could buy her a drink.

The young lady introduced herself as Olivia Phillips and said she would love a gin and tonic but on the condition that she was allowed to join him whilst she drank it. Sitting together, Olivia was the chattier of the two, asking George what he was reading and which college he was in. In return, if somewhat unimaginatively, he asked the same questions of her; she was in her first year reading English and she was at Lady Margaret Hall. Although George knew she would not have been in the bar unless she had attended the Union debate that evening, he still asked if she had attended it.

After confirming that she had, she asked him which way he had voted.

"I voted against the motion. What about you?"

She ducked his question and posed another one for him.

"Did you vote against the motion because of the merits of the arguments put forward against it or because you were going to vote against it come what may?"

"I went to the debate with a reasonably open mind although, if the voting had taken place before any of the debating, I'd have voted against. Nothing I heard from those arguing the case for conscription was sufficient to make me change my view, so I voted against. What about you?"

"I voted against as well. But I don't think a vote taken at the Oxford Union will make any difference in the long run. If our members of parliament think it is necessary, they'll introduce it even if none of them will ever have to sign up."

"But don't you think that they'll only do that if it really is necessary?"

"It would be nice to think that. But I don't think declaring war just because Germany invaded Belgium was absolutely necessary. So who knows?"

"That sounds rather pessimistic; surely those in power have families and even if they're not forced to sign up, they'll be affected if those close to them are."

"I suppose that's possible but I'm more inclined to think that politicians are less interested in their families and more interested in how the public perceives them."

"That's a rather cynical view, isn't it?"

"It probably sounds like one but it isn't meant to be."

George enjoyed talking to Olivia. She was a woman with a mind of her own and he admired that. Noticing she had nearly finished her drink, he asked her if he could buy her another one. Turning down his offer disappointed him until she said that it was her turn to buy. George accepted her offer to buy him a drink on the condition that he went to the bar to order them.

Waiting at the bar for his order to be taken gave George time to think about what next to talk to her about. He would steer clear of politics and the War; asking her views of the Suffragette movement was too close to politics so he would keep away from that – that could wait for another time if there was to be one. He could ask her about her family but he wanted to come up with something more interesting to talk about; or he could ask her about her school but that was hardly original - she had probably been asked that by every man she had spoken to since arriving at university. Once back at their table and before asking her about the books she was studying for her course, she asked him about his family and why he had chosen to go to Oxford. The more they talked the more George found himself being captivated by her; never before had he met a woman so relaxed in the presence of male company or with whom he found himself so at ease. After finishing their second drinks, she told him it was time for her to return to her rooms in college. He offered to walk her back but she said that would not be necessary. As they were parting, he was not sure how to tell her that he hoped they could meet again; anticipating that might be the case, she asked if he had visited yet the city's Ashmolean Museum. As neither of them had, she asked if he would like to accompany her that weekend on a visit. Before heading back to their colleges, they agreed to meet at the museum's main entrance at 3 o'clock on the following Saturday afternoon.

As they set off in opposite directions heading back to their respective colleges, George found it difficult to keep the smile off his face. He had thoroughly enjoyed meeting and talking to Olivia but wondered whether she had enjoyed herself as much; he knew the university's female students were significantly outnumbered by the male students so there was much more choice for Olivia to decide which male company she wanted to keep than there was for him to choose the female company he wanted to keep. He knew that he wanted to see her again and hoped she felt the same about him but he had no idea how to make her want to spend more time with him than with any of the other numerous male students at university.

There were two full days for George to kill before their next meeting. The thought of seeing Olivia again was starting to pre-occupy him, not least because he was anxious to make a good impression when they met again. He did not want to come across to Olivia as someone who knew very little about art, a subject in which he had shown little interest to date. In order to overcome this and allow him to give her the impression he knew something about art, he decided to make a quick tour of the museum the day before they were due to meet.

The contents of the museum were more extensive than George imagined and the quick tour took much more time than he had expected; it left him feeling more confident about his next visit in the company of Olivia, hopeful that he would not come across as as much of a philistine as would otherwise have been the case.

George spent much of the Saturday morning nervously worrying himself about his afternoon rendezvous with Olivia. Even though the museum was no more than a ten minute walk from college, he set off in plenty of time, arriving five minutes early. Five minutes later there was no sign of Olivia and he started to worry that she might have forgotten or changed her mind. When she was ten minutes late, he started thinking how much longer he would wait before giving up; he could always go into the museum on his own but, as he had been round the museum the day before, there was no point in doing that. He suddenly noticed Olivia, turning into Beaumont Street as she made her way to the museum. She apologised to him for being a few minutes late but, because of his pleasure and relief at seeing her, he did not hear, or even care, what her reason for being late was.

They spent the next two hours together admiring the wonderful collection of art at the museum, both very relaxed in each other's company. George did not volunteer too much information about the collection for fear it would appear he had just read up on it and instead displayed no more knowledge than he thought would be sufficient to suggest an interest in art.

After the museum tour, they adjourned to one of the tearooms nearby, one popular with students. Much as he was keen to spend as much time as possible with her, he did not want to appear too keen and, after they had finished their tea, asked Olivia when she had to be back in college by.

"As I'm signed in for college dinner, I have to be back by 7 o'clock. If I'd signed out, I could've stayed out until 10 o'clock."

"As I have nothing on this evening, would you mind if I walked you back to college?"

"I'd like that very much if you don't mind."

"I'd be delighted to."

As they approached Olivia's college, he asked her if he could meet up with her again. Olivia said she would like that and, as both their diaries were clear the following day, they agreed to have lunch together in one of the pubs by the river.

Over the course of the rest of the term, they saw each other at least twice a week. They usually met up once at the weekend and once during the week and, by the time their first term was coming to an end, they both knew a lot more about each other. By then, George had learned that Olivia was the oldest of three sisters and her father was the headmaster of a boys' school in Sussex; Olivia had been a day-girl at a school nearby but living at her father's school with so many boys all around meant that she felt entirely at ease in the presence of male company, unlike so many of her contemporaries from school, particularly those without brothers. Olivia had also learnt about George's family, that his only sibling was a younger brother and his father worked on the Stock Exchange in the City of London.

On their last evening together before the end of term, they discussed whether they would be able to meet up during the vacation but it seemed unlikely. If Olivia were to come to London to see George, he would have to tell his parents about Olivia, whose existence they were unaware of; and she was reluctant to invite him to her home because she thought that, apart from herself, there was not enough there to interest him. As their final evening together came to a close, George walked Olivia back to her college. He promised her he would write during the holidays; she said she would like that before bidding him goodnight with a kiss on his lips. The kiss was over quickly but not too quickly and he would have liked it to have lasted longer but, never having previously experienced anything quite as intimate, he did not know what he should have done to prolong the pleasure. Previous evenings out had ended with no more than a kiss on the cheek and he had been contented enough with that but, on his way back to college that night, he convinced himself their relationship was heading in a more serious direction.

After two weeks apart, George wrote to Olivia but, never having written to a girl before, was unsure what to write. He missed her and he would tell her that but surely she would want to hear more about what he was up to; at the same time, he did not want his letter to be merely a recount of what he had been up to since he had come down at the end of term. Much as he longed to see her again, anything too passionate like a love letter would be inappropriate at this stage of their relationship and more likely to put her off him. After tearing up numerous attempts at a letter, he finally settled on what to write. Three pages would be enough, not too long or too short. The letter started with enquiring how she was and went on to what he had been up to. He expressed views about the state of the War; with the First Battle of Ypres having come to an end as winter weather set in with neither side gaining the upper hand and both sides suffering heavy casualties, George expressed the view that fighting would resume sometime in the Spring but, with neither side gaining much in the way of territory, it was going to take much longer for the War to end than the politicians were predicting. He ended the letter saying that he was missing her and was very much looking forward to seeing her again next term, signing it off "With love" and a couple of kisses, uncertain how she would react to this.

The letter arrived at Olivia's home two days later. Her mother handed her the envelope when Olivia returned home from the tuition class she had been giving to one of the pupils from her former school; by the time she was handed the envelope, her two younger sisters knew there was a letter for her and were keen to know who it was from.

"Is it from a friend or an admirer?" enquired Georgia, the younger of Olivia's two younger sisters.

"How do I know who it's from when I haven't even opened it?" came Olivia's terse reply.

"Well, open it up and then you can tell me."

Olivia opened the envelope and, even though she had told Georgia she did not know who the sender was, she knew it was from George, as she was hoping and expecting it would be. On confirming it was from George, Olivia told her sister that it was from both a friend and admirer. Being a younger sister, Georgia wanted to know more about the sender of the letter but Olivia was only willing to let her know that he was a friend from university.

Seeing the letter was from George, Olivia wanted to read it in private so went to her room. When she had been at school, she had received numerous letters from boys but they were always from boys at her father's school, most of whom wanted to vent their frustrations caused by being locked up in an institution with no other female company around. Receiving a letter from George was different; she wanted to hear from him and to hear his news. Reading his letter made her long to see him again; it saddened her that she would not be seeing him for another three weeks but pleased her to know that he was missing her. She too was missing him and it was reassuring to know that he felt the same way about her.

Over dinner that evening, Olivia's mother asked her about the letter; coming from her mother, it was more out of genuine interest than would have been the case had it come from one of her sisters, who would use it as ammunition with which to tease her.

"He's just someone I have met at university; he's reading classics and we've seen each other every once in a while."

"Will we get the chance to meet him and what's his name?" asked her mother.

"He's called George but I hardly know him so it's much too early to say whether you'll meet him. Anyway, I doubt he'd want to meet my sisters."

"Why not?" her mother replied.

"Because they're so childish and wouldn't know how to behave in front of a charming young man. They'd just behave like giggling schoolgirls."

"Not necessarily; it might show them how they should behave if ever they have boyfriends of their own."

"Not much chance of them ever having boyfriends, is there?" replied Olivia in a rather puerile tone.

"Now Olivia, you're being the silly one. Of course they will one day. So, will we get a chance to meet him?"

"Mother, I hardly know him so it's much too early to invite him to come and visit us. I'll just have to see how things go next term; if things go well, maybe he can come and stay with us in the next holidays or perhaps in the summer. We'll just have to see."

Her mother knew from the tetchiness in Olivia's voice that that was, at least for the time being, enough on the subject of George. Keen to discuss something which was more likely to be of interest to her husband, she enquired of him what news there was of boys from the school who were amongst the war casualties. Although a depressing subject to talk about, it was something they did not shy away from as they felt a bond with all leavers, having been *in loco parentis* to the boys for much of their adolescent years; any casualty, however minor, was hard for them to take but the loss of life of any of their boys, at such a young age, left such a hollow feeling. With neither side able to achieve a breakthrough before they dug in for the winter, the lull in fighting meant that there was no news of any more casualties but, with the lives of nine of the school's former pupils having already been taken, that was only small consolation.

Olivia posted her reply to George three days later. She thanked him for his letter and told him how pleased she was to hear his news. She did not write much about what she had been up to as she wanted to save it for him for when they next saw each other. She too finished her letter saying she was missing him, although she did not admit how much and that she was looking forward to seeing him again once term started in less than three weeks' time.

Not having made any arrangements with Olivia where to meet when they were both back at university, the day after he was back George went to Olivia's college to see whether she was back. The porter at her college informed him that she had not returned to college yet but assured George that the note he left for her would be handed to her on her return. Olivia received the note the next day and two days later she met George for lunch at the same pub they had been to the day after their first outing together to the museum. Not wanting to be late for their reunion, George arrived a few minutes early and was relieved that Olivia arrived more or less on time this time. As she approached him, he was not sure how to greet her but fortunately she took any indecision on his part away as she walked across to him, threw her arms around him and planted a kiss on his lips more passionate than, and every bit as intimate as, the one when they had said their goodbyes at the end of the previous term.

They were both excited to see each other again. They clearly enjoyed each other's company, their time apart during the university holidays only making them want to be together more. In order not to allow their relationship to distract them from their studies and from the other extra-curricular opportunities which university life offered, they agreed to restrict the time they saw each other to no more than two or three times a week.

Much as they both missed each other when they were not together, it did mean that, when they did see each other again, the greeting kisses lasted longer and stirred in both of them a desire for more intimacy. However neither of them knew how to satisfy such desire as they rarely found themselves alone anywhere private; university rules meant that they could not visit each other in their rooms in college so, whenever they met, it was usually in a public place.

Life continued like this for the rest of their first year at university together and, as the summer term drew to an end, they knew they did not want the summer holiday period to pass without seeing each other. Thinking it more likely that her parents would agree to her visiting George at his family home if they had met him first, the two of them agreed George would pay a visit to her home first. So, by the time they went their separate ways at the end of their first year at university, their plans for the summer vacation had been made - provided their parents agreed to it, George would be introduced to Olivia's family and stay with them for a few days in July and a few weeks later she would stay with George and his family.

With neither of them having any difficulty persuading their parents to agree to it, George went to stay with Olivia and her family for three days at the beginning of July. Travelling by train, Olivia met him at the railway station nearest to her home; her father had offered to drive to the station to collect him, but she wanted to be on her own when George disembarked from his train. Olivia was at the station in good time before his train was due to arrive and, with the train being on time, did not have long to wait. The two of them travelled by bus from the railway station to her nearest village, before completing the final mile of the journey to her home on foot. Despite Olivia's assurances that he had nothing to worry about, he was still nervous about meeting her family; this was a new experience for him and he was keen to win their approval. She told him just to be himself and everything would be fine.

Olivia's sisters were not, as she feared they might be, silly or giggly in front of him and he found Olivia's parents easy and interesting to talk to; being a headmaster, her father was used to conversing with young men and was interested to hear George's views on a wide range of subjects. Inevitably, they discussed the War and, perhaps with his school leavers in mind, Olivia's father was keen to hear an opinion about volunteering from someone George's age. George felt that Olivia's father genuinely wanted to hear his opinion rather than test his patriotism. Olivia's father appeared to respect George's opinion on the subject because he recognised that he had given serious thought to it and, in coming to his view, George had weighed up the arguments for and against.

"Sir, for so long as there is a choice, I think ultimately the decision to volunteer must be left to the individual. I also strongly believe that, before anyone decides to volunteer, they should have a clear understanding of what they're volunteering for and what that involves. Sadly though, although I appreciate there may be good reasons for it, not enough information is given about the conditions volunteers will have to endure and the chances of them not surviving. I believe many lives have been lost and will continue to be lost and, for many of those, they will do so without fully understanding the risks they were taking on board. Unwise decisions from superiors less affected have resulted in too little being gained for the losses suffered."

"So George, does that mean you will not volunteer?"

"Sir, I chose not to volunteer before starting at Oxford. I can still volunteer but I have chosen not to. I would like to finish my time at university first before deciding whether or not to enlist. I may be of more use to the war effort with a degree behind me. I fear though that the choice may well be taken out of my hands well before I shall have graduated."

"Why d'you think that?"

"Sir, it's close to a year now since Britain declared war. What have we achieved in that time? We have stopped Germany advancing as far as the Channel but we have not forced them out of Belgium. And that has all come at a huge cost in terms of lives. Both sides now seem to be well-entrenched and I just don't see the War ending soon. The longer it continues the more pressure will be put on our government to force young men like myself to serve their country. And should that happen as I think it will, I shall have no choice but to serve."

"If one of my pupils asked me if I thought he should volunteer, what d'you think I should say?"

"I think you should tell him that, before making any decision, he should look into exactly what it entails and weigh up the risks involved with fighting on the front line against the likely consequences of not volunteering. I would advise him to ask himself whether, for the sake of his country, he is willing to make what may be the ultimate sacrifice."

"And d'you think it is fair to label someone who does not volunteer a coward?"

"I don't think so provided they can justify their reasons for not volunteering. If a young man says he is not willing to fight because he is against the War in principle, that doesn't make him a coward."

"George, I shall bear in mind what you say if my advice is sought."

George had no idea what Olivia had planned, if anything, for his three-day stay with her and her family. Over breakfast on the first morning after his arrival, she told him they were going to play some tennis with her sisters. George knew he could not say no but he had hardly ever played tennis before, his only experience of playing it being limited to a few knock-ups with friends whilst at school.

George warned Olivia that he was not very good at tennis but was willing to give it a go. Despite being the worst on court, he enjoyed the tennis and, by the time they had played two sets, he felt that he was getting the hang of it and even showing signs of improvement. Olivia and her sisters were much better than he had expected them to be, all of them benefitting from having access to the school's two grass tennis courts. Keen to improve, George asked Olivia if he could play some more tennis after lunch and she was more than willing to oblige. Having played tennis since she was a child, Olivia explained to George how he could improve his game and, by the time they had spent an hour on court, she could see there was more potential in his tennis than had been apparent when he had first appeared on court that morning.

Her plans for the next day did not include tennis despite George's keenness to play but instead involved a cycle ride to the coast for a picnic on the beach, weather permitting. The beach at Climping was only ten miles away and at this time of year, the sea should be warm enough for them to swim.

The weather the next day did not let them down and, after Olivia's mother had prepared and packed a picnic, they set off on their bicycles. After peddling their way through quiet country roads, they reached the beach soon after midday. Despite the sunny weather, the beach was almost deserted but Olivia suggested they picnic further down the beach; with the tide going out, they cycled on the wet sand and found an ideal picnic spot about half a mile down the beach. They laid out a rug on the soft sand just above the high tide mark but, before tucking into their lunch, took a quick dip in the sea to cool off and freshen themselves up after their cycle ride.

Olivia had come better prepared than George who had only his shorts to swim in whereas she had her swimming costume on under the dress she had been cycling in. The sea was bracing but it was an ideal temperature for refreshing them after their morning excursion. After a few minutes splashing around, they retreated to their picnic rug and lay down to dry off and enjoy the sunshine before seeing what was in the picnic basket.

"So what d'you make of my family?" asked Olivia as she was lying next to George with her eyes closed.

"Your parents have been most welcoming and have made me feel very easy. Your sisters are very sweet and both rather good at tennis. That leaves just you. You make me very happy and I miss you when we're not together."

"George, d'you love me?" Olivia asked teasingly.

"Olivia, we've now known each other for over nine months. Over that time, I have never felt happier and the more I see you the more I want to be with you. I have never thought of my feelings for you in terms of whether or not I love you but now that you ask, I can say that, yes, I do think I love you."

Olivia knew George well enough to know that this was about as committed as he was ever like to be when it came to expressing his emotions; it was just the way he was that he had to say he thought he was in love with her, rather than that he was in love with her as if he did not know what love really felt like. She knew he was really admitting he was in love with her but she thought she might try and pry a bit more out of him.

"What d'you mean, you think you love me? Don't you know if you love me?"

George could not tell if she had been upset by his answer but, without ever having loved a woman before, he was not sure what love was. He thought his answer was honest enough and he had not expected Olivia to question him on it.

"Olivia, I had never loved any woman before I met you. I have never wanted to be with a woman more than I have wanted to be with you. As far as I know, I am in love with you."

Olivia was of course delighted to hear this but she could not resist one last effort to get him to say he loved her.

"Does that mean you love me?"

"Yes, Olivia, it means I love you."

With that, Olivia leaned over towards George and thanked him and, as if to celebrate the first time he had told her he loved her, she kissed him on his lips before telling him she loved him as well and that it was now time for lunch.

After lunch, they both sun-bathed on the rug, dozing off in the heat. When they were both awake, they decided it was time for another swim. Both were surprised how much the sun had warmed up the sea as the tide was going out but after a good fifteen minutes in the water, Olivia said she thought they should think about drying off before heading back home.

As they ambled their way back up the beach, George challenged Olivia to a race.

"Race you back to our picnic rug."

Olivia started running back towards the rug without answering in an attempt to gain an advantage but George was just fast enough to catch her up and be the first to reach the rug, collapsing on it as he did so. Arriving at the rug only seconds later, she collapsed on the rug on top of George as he lay there. Seeing that there was no one else in sight, she smothered his face with kisses as she lay on top of him and, as she did so, could feel the effect this was having on him. Rather than being embarrassed by what she could feel as she pressed her body closer to George, she did not want to waste this moment, a moment that offered her a rare opportunity for more intimacy. As she moved her body away from him, she placed her hands on his bare stomach and then to the top of his wet shorts. George lay there as if frozen as she unbuckled the top of his shorts before reaching inside to touch what only seconds earlier she had felt pressing against her body.

George was left speechless by Olivia's actions. He had no idea what to do or say. He was worried that someone might see them but he also did not want Olivia to stop what she was doing. It was eventually Olivia who broke the silence.

"George, I hope you don't mind me touching you like that. I know that I shouldn't but I so want to touch you and feel you and that means all of you. You make me feel like that. I'm sorry if you think I'm being too forward but I cannot help myself."

"Of course I don't mind. The pleasure you make me feel is such a new experience for me and I'm not sure what I should say when you make me feel like that. I just hope I can make you feel the same way."

"You do make me feel wonderful just being with you. And it's even more wonderful when we have time together just the two of us. We shall just have to find ways of doing this more often."

After a couple of minutes lying next to each other, Olivia said they should think about heading home soon because, as she told George, she would not want her parents to start worrying about them or what they might have been up to.

As she moved away from his body, she gave him one last kiss before they packed everything up and headed back down the beach on their bicycles for the journey home.

Olivia's mother had a cup of tea waiting for them when they returned home. Enquiring how their day had been she was told how much they had enjoyed the picnic she had so kindly made for them and what a lovely time they had had. By the time they had all finished their dinner that evening, Olivia and George were feeling tired from their cycling and time in the sun but they were keen not to retire for the night before everyone else. Not long after 10 o'clock, Olivia's parents decided it was bedtime for them and that was a cue for everyone to else to retire for the night.

Although George was feeling worn out, he found it difficult to get to sleep; his mind was racing as he thought about the day's events and the way Olivia had touched him that afternoon. He finally dozed off only to be woken not long after when he heard his bedroom door opening. In the darkness he could not make out who was there but, after hearing the door being shut, he could make out quiet footsteps in his room. He knew not to ask who was there because it was obvious and within seconds after he heard the door shut, the sheets and blankets on his bed were pulled back as Olivia climbed into bed next to him. Much as he wanted this, he was worried that Olivia's parents were still awake or heard her tiptoeing down the upstairs corridor from her bedroom to the room where George was staying.

"Are you sure this is safe? What will your parents do if they find out?"

"My father is snoring away and, even if that is keeping my mother awake, she would not have heard me above that noise."

"What about your sisters? What will they think?"

"They're asleep. Anyway, what has it got to do with them? We just have to make sure we keep the noise down and don't disturb any of them."

Olivia's answers did not reassure George. Despite feeling most uncomfortable at the thought of being caught in bed with Olivia, in her parents' home, he was not minded to ask her to return to her room.

As if to stop him from talking, Olivia kissed him on his lips and, as she did so, lifted her nightdress above her waist. Being in a single bed, they could not avoid almost every part of their bodies touching and George could not hide the effect this had on him; before he knew it, Olivia had untied the tops of his pyjamas. As she tried to remove them, she was only able to lower his pyjamas to his knees before he kicked them off leaving nothing between them below their waists. The feel of Olivia's skin against his made George want to touch her with his hands; Olivia offered no resistance as his hands caressed her back before finding their way down to her buttocks and then to her stomach. Olivia parted her legs slightly as if to encourage him to touch her there; as he started stroking her pubic hair, George could tell from her reaction that she was enjoying it. Olivia guided his hand between her legs and, even if he was unsure what he should do next, she knew exactly what she was doing. As she moved her body up and down, he could tell from her every movement that she did not want him to stop. Her movements were causing the springs on the bed to creak but she was too carried away to worry about that. It was not long though before Olivia let out a sigh and slumped herself against George, unable to take any more.

"George, you make me feel so good. I didn't want you to stop. I have never felt like that before."

George did not know what to say. Pleased as he was to make Olivia feel the way she did, he was still concerned that her parents were going to storm in and find Olivia in bed with him.

"Olivia, it's pleasing to know that I make you feel like you do. I only wish I could feel more relaxed and not worry about your parents hearing us or catching us. We must find a way to spend a night together without having to worry about being found out."

"Perhaps I should go back to my room to ease your worries."

"I don't want you to leave but I think it is probably best. I can't promise it'll be any easier when you come and stay with my parents but it is something we can both look forward to."

On that note, Olivia gave him one final kiss for the night before tiptoeing her way back to her room, keeping the noise to a minimum.

The following morning George bade his farewells to Olivia's family before setting off back home. Olivia came to visit him three weeks later and stayed for a couple of nights. On one of their two days together they cycled through Richmond Park to Kew Gardens before returning to Barnes along the towpath next to the river and on the other day they paid a visit to the British Museum. Staying in George's family home did not give them the same opportunities to be alone together as had been the case when staying in Olivia's family home; frustrating as this was, there was nothing they could do about it and they were both just thankful to be together.

It was another four weeks before they returned to university and saw each other again. In the meantime, they wrote to each other and agreed the dates they would return to university and where next to meet.

The first term back at university in their second year followed much the same pattern as their first year, with George and Olivia meeting up once during the week and again at the weekends. As a result of his stay with Olivia's family, George took it upon himself to improve his tennis and he and Olivia often played tennis together at the weekend. Finding private moments to themselves continued to prove difficult, George not being permitted to visit Olivia in her room in college; the men's colleges were not so strict about young ladies visiting although Olivia always felt the porters at the entrance to George's college talked about her behind her back and frowned upon the frequency of her visits. Even when she made her way to George's room, they could never be certain that one of George's friends would not suddenly burst in uninvited.

Before the term was over, George, along with all the other students in his college, received a letter from the Earl of Derby, the Government's Director-General of Recruiting, requiring him to declare whether or not he would enlist. George's view about enlisting had not changed whilst at university and he therefore refused the Government's request to enlist. He felt though that it would be just a matter of time before he would be required to enlist so, as far as George was concerned, his refusal to do so was little more than buying a bit more time before having to fight.

The passing of the Military Service Bill in January 1916 forced George's hand. George was anxious to avoid being sent to the trenches to fight after hearing accounts of the conditions there and the high casualty rates. He decided the best way he could avoid this would be to join an army medical corps but, without any medical training, this was not an option; he considered joining the Friends Ambulance Unit, but rejected the idea because he was neither a Quaker nor a registered conscientious objector. This left him with the choice of either the Royal Navy or enlisting in the Royal Flying Corps. The Royal Navy did not appeal as much as the Royal Flying Corps because the chances of survival seemed worse in the Navy; furthermore, in the Royal Flying Corps, it might be possible to undertake aerial photographic reconnaissance, thereby minimising the risk of enemy attack.

Before he would decide, George wanted to discuss the options not only with Olivia but also his parents and his brother Edward, who would also be required to enlist. Olivia was only too aware that, whatever his decision, he would be putting his life at risk and, in her view, survival was a matter of luck as it depended so much on whether or not you were in the wrong place at the wrong time; and whether or not you were in the wrong place at the wrong time was more or less at the whim of the those not putting their own lives at risk.

After discussing the matter with his family and Olivia, George stuck with his initial idea and decided to enlist with the Royal Flying Corps; the only argument put to him as to why he should not enlist with them was his lack of flying experience but that was the same not only for all those enlisting in the Royal Flying Corps but also for those who would be serving with the Imperial German Flying Corps.

After the Military Service Bill came into force in March 1916, he enlisted in the newly-formed No. 46 Squadron of the Royal Flying Corps, based at Wyton Aerodrome near Huntingdon.

Because he was still at university, George was permitted to finish his second year at university before reporting for duty at Wyton.

He tried as best he could to ensure that the last term of his second year at university was not over-shadowed by what lay ahead and spent as much time as he could in the company of Olivia.

They had been going out together over eighteen months and they had discussed marriage, not least because marriage would have excused George from enlisting, at least for the time being. However, they both agreed that, were they to marry, it would have to be because they both wanted to and not for some other motive, such as to avoid having to enlist.

The summer term passed all too quickly and only two weeks after the term was over George left home bound for Wyton. He spent those last two weeks with Olivia, one of them when he went to stay with her family and the other when she stayed with his. Finally, she travelled with him to King's Cross where, after a tearful farewell, he boarded the train to Huntingdon, a little over three miles from the RFC base at Wyton. As she watched the train pull out of the station, Olivia wondered when she would see him again. Hopefully, he would be given leave before too long.

On arrival at Wyton, George discovered that he was one of eighteen who had volunteered to join the squadron. None of them had any experience of flying and only six of them had ever driven a car. Barely three weeks after joining up, they found themselves in the air for the first time. The squadron had acquired a couple of two-seater Nieuport 12 planes which they used for training and instructors took each of the volunteers up as often as the weather allowed. Flying with the instructors involved not merely learning how to fly the plane but understanding the plane's capacity and capabilities and learning navigational skills. Less than two months after his first flying lesson, George found himself flying solo. Some of the new recruits were filled with fear at the prospect but he had enjoyed his flying lessons and, although he knew he still had much to learn, was excited to fly solo for the first time. The flight went without incident. He only flew for twenty minutes but, in that time, he appreciated how easy it could be to lose one's bearings. Fortunately, a clear sky meant that visibility was good and a lack of wind prevented him from being blown off course but less benign weather conditions would be much more testing.

Four months after joining up with his squadron George was granted his first leave. In that four month period, he had had to learn fast but, after every flight, he felt he had learnt something new. Some of his landings had been bumpier than others, particularly when landing in windier conditions and, on more than one occasion, clouds had appeared unexpectedly, causing him to lose sight of the ground below him – the planes had no navigational devices so the pilots had to rely on following the railway lines and other features to determine their whereabouts and when cloud cover made that impossible, they often had difficulty in locating their airdrome. Most of them experienced some problem with the engines during their training which caused them anxious moments but the more they coped with such problems the more confidence it gave them and they understood better the strengths and weaknesses of the planes they were flying.

George took his leave over a weekend in October. He caught the train to London on the Friday and spent the night with his parents before catching the train the next day to Oxford; his brother Edward was not at home as he too had volunteered and was training at the Royal Military Academy at Sandhurst for a commission in the Army.

George knew he had to spend some time with his parents before rushing off to see Olivia, so it was not until the afternoon on the Saturday when he met up with her. They had agreed to meet at the Randolph Hotel. Over tea, she was interested to hear all about his training to date as the idea of flying sounded so exciting but she did not want to think about what it could lead to and the inevitable posting abroad. As it was the weekend, she was able to spend the whole of it with him without having to worry about lectures and work and she was thrilled when he told her over tea that he had booked a double room in the hotel for the night. He had not been sure how she would react to this or whether she would think him too presumptuous for inviting her to spend the night with him – but at worst, she could always refuse his invitation.

"George, that's very sweet of you. I shall have to go back to college and tell the porter I shall be out for the night."

She went back to her college, packed an overnight bag and got back to the hotel as quickly as she could. Meanwhile he reserved a table for dinner for the two of them and waited at the hotel.

Before dinner, they went to the hotel bar; the excitement of spending the night together for the first time had the effect of stifling any other conversation until a second drink made them both feel more relaxed. George asked about Olivia's family and her university work and, although she had not wanted to talk about it earlier, she was now more prepared to hear about what lay in store for George.

"George, there's part of me that doesn't want to know if you'll be posted abroad to fight because, if I knew you had to, it would make me fear the worst but, at the same time, I'm desperate to know because not knowing is just as bad. Have you been given any indication whether or not you'll have to go to France or Belgium?"

"The training we've been undertaking is obviously for a purpose and whatever that purpose is, I can't imagine it's one that will be of much help to the war effort if we stay in England. I think, even though we haven't been told it, it's inevitable that we'll be sent to France or Belgium at some stage."

"Assuming you are sent, do you know what you'll do there?"

"The planes are being used mostly to carry out reconnaissance work from the air. They're flying over enemy territory to obtain information and report back on the strengths and weaknesses of enemy positions."

"Is that risky?"

He hesitated before replying. The risks included coping with adverse weather conditions, possible engine failure and being shot at from the ground; however, increasingly, the War was being fought in the skies as the warring forces started to develop equipment which would allow machine guns to be fired from the planes and which allowed the planes to drop bombs but he did not think now was the time to worry her about all of that.

"There'll always be risks involved when flying aeroplanes, in the same way there are risks when driving cars. I'll feel less at risk though than those who are fighting on the ground, who are well within range of enemy fire."

"I know it sounds silly but I won't be able not to worry about you. I don't worry about you when you're flying in England even though I suppose there are risks involved in that but that seems so far removed from the battlefields. Once you're flying near enemy lines, it just feels so much more dangerous."

"I do understand. I worry in much the same way about what will happen to my brother when he gets his commission. He'll be exposing himself to the risks I've deliberately avoided by joining up with the Flying Corps. It's time we went through for dinner and no more talk about the future unless it is about the two of us."

They finished their drinks and made their way to the dining room. Other than afternoon tea, neither of them had eaten at the Randolph Hotel before and the menu offered them much more choice than they were used to. Both started with soup and, for the main course, Olivia ordered fish and George the steak-and-kidney pie. He also ordered a bottle of wine with the meal and once the meal was finished, a glass of port for himself. Olivia had had enough to drink and hoped that the glass of port was not one glass too many for George. Just as he finished his port and before he had time to order another glass, she suggested it was time they retired to their room. She did not want to spend what was going to be her first night with a man with one who was too tipsy; she wanted it to be memorable for the both of them.

Even though they had shared a bed together, albeit only briefly when George had stayed with Olivia's family, spending the night with someone else was a new experience for them both. As they undressed, neither was sure what to say to the other and the silence continued once in bed together whilst they embraced, before eventually drifting off to sleep. George woke in the morning before Olivia; as he lay there with Olivia still asleep, he stared at her, not wanting to disturb her as she lay breathing quietly with a contented smile on her face. He hoped that her look reflected how she really felt.

When Olivia eventually woke, she saw George looking at her.

"What are you looking at?"

"Someone I can't take my eyes off."

Olivia reached across to George and kissed him.

"What have you got planned for today?"

George had nothing planned other than to catch the train back to London later that afternoon.

"Nothing other than to spend as much of it as possible with you. What have you got planned?"

"Nothing either. I can put off my work until tomorrow. Actually, at the moment, I'm not in any hurry to get out of bed."

It was just before midday that George and Olivia emerged from their hotel room. Having missed breakfast, they chose to head straight off for lunch at the Perch, an inn close to the Thames. The walk along the river to the inn would take them a little over thirty minutes but allow them to be there before it became too crowded. When they arrived at the inn, they found a table close to the log fire which was burning away and bringing warmth back to their bodies after their walk.

Knowing that their time together was running out, on the way back to Oxford after lunch they walked more slowly as if it would prolong their time together; they returned to the hotel to collect their bags before making their way to the station for George to catch his train.

Before boarding his train, Olivia asked George when he might next be granted leave, anxious to know when they might next see each other.

"I honestly don't know. I'm not even sure those in charge of my squadron know when we might be posted abroad. If we are still in England at Christmas, I hope we'll have some time off then."

"George, I know that is less than three months away but it still seems such a long way off. Let's hope we don't have to wait that long to be with each other again."

"Let's hope so. Let's also hope that, if I do have time off then, we shall be able to spend a night together like last night."

"We will because I know we will want to make it happen."

She kissed him before telling him it was time for him to go. As the train pulled out, he waved back and she blew one last kiss towards him.

George spent the Sunday night with his parents, arriving back at Wyton the following day. Waiting for him on his return was a notice requiring all members of the squadron to attend a meeting at seven o'clock that evening in the mess hall.

George did not want to speculate with other members of the squadron why they were being summonsed; they would find out soon enough and, in his mind, there was nothing to be gained by any such speculation. All members of the squadron other than the squadron leader were in the mess hall at the time they were required to be there, the squadron leader arriving on the dot of 7:00 p.m. to address those present.

"Gentlemen, I shall come straight to the point. We have received orders from above to relocate to an aerodrome in France. The aerodrome is located just outside a village called La Gorgue which is some twenty miles south of Ypres and we shall be based nearby in Arras. I have not received any information about what our duties will be when we get there – they will no doubt become much clearer once we are there. We are due to move out of our base here by the end of this week. Any questions?"

A number of George's colleagues asked questions about how they would be transferred there and how close their new base was to the enemy lines, all of which the squadron leader answered. Foremost on George's mind was the wish to let his family and Olivia know about his relocation.

"Sir, can you please let us know if we can share this information with anyone?"

"Each of you can tell your immediate family that you are being posted to France but you are not at liberty at this stage to inform them exactly where in France. You will have the opportunity to tell them that once you are there."

George did not want to ask about whether he would be able to tell Olivia as well for fear of being told he could not. Instead, he decided that he would ask his parents to tell her about his new whereabouts.

By the end of the week, the squadron was ready to leave for France. The flying of the squadron's planes to their new base was left to the most senior airmen whilst George and the seventeen others in the squadron who had volunteered at the same time as him made the journey to Arras by train to the south coast, then by ferry across the Channel and finally in trucks to their final destination. Before his departure, George wrote to his parents telling them of his new posting and requesting that they also pass the news on to Olivia. That he was being posted abroad did not come as a shock to his parents but it was still not welcome news; they had believed it was inevitable but that did not provide them with any comfort. They feared that it would not be long before Edward, their other son, would also be posted abroad and, much as they tried not to think about it, there was always a fear at the back of their minds that their two boys might never return.

On receiving George's letter, his parents discussed how to let Olivia know. Eventually, agreeing it would come best from his mother, Alice wrote to Olivia to tell her the news of George's posting and promised to keep her informed as soon as they heard any news from him. Olivia's reaction on hearing of George's posting was different to that of his parents; it never crossed her mind that he would not come back and all she could think about, without knowing the answer, was when she would see him again.

In many ways, life in France was similar to life at Wyton, with the pilots continuing their flying exercises in much the same way. The most noticeable differences were the noise from the front line and the landscape.

Even a lull in the fighting did not prevent the occasional artillery bombardment and, with the front line less than ten miles away from the aerodrome, the shelling was all too audible. The major battles that had already taken place close to the border between Belgium and France had also left their mark, destroying much of what had been farmland and woods.

Another significant difference was the pilots were now flying over land occupied by the enemy; no longer could they land where they liked in the knowledge that a safe landing would leave them in safe hands. Most of the time George spent flying was on reconnaissance missions, trying to monitor any movement of enemy troops and to ascertain the strength of the German front line and the support lines providing back-up; others in George's squadron were tasked with carrying out aerial photographic work, to provide the Allied forces with better information about the lay of the land if ever they were successful in forcing the German army back.

Although George was conscious of the risks in flying over enemy territory, it did not unduly concern him and he was relieved that he was not in the firing line in the way the troops in the trenches beneath him were. By now, he had flown enough to feel confident in the air. The risk of being hit by ground fire was minimal and he was confident that, should he come across any German planes on similar missions, he would have no difficulty in getting back to La Gorgue. Despite his growing confidence, he knew he could not afford to be complacent or inadequately prepared for unforeseen events. His knowledge of his plane's capacity came to his rescue on one particular occasion when his engine stalled and he had to rely upon a favourable wind blowing from the right direction to get him safely back to La Gorgue. On another occasion, whilst flying closer than normal to enemy aircraft carrying out routine photography close to the front line, the photographer in the German aircraft suddenly and unexpectedly swapped his camera for a revolver and started firing it at him; he was able to take evasive action before any damage was done but it taught him a useful lesson – do not take anything for granted.

The winter of 1916 was a severe one and, with snow on the ground, flying came to a halt. The snow also brought the fighting in the trenches to a temporary end. With the adverse weather conditions looking set to last several weeks, George was allowed a week's leave at the beginning of January. Getting back to England in such conditions was far from straightforward, but George was determined to do so. Most of his colleagues were happy enough taking their leave in Paris and enjoying the nightlife Paris had to offer to take their minds off the War but the only thing on

George's mind was spending as much of his leave with Olivia as he could, even if that meant as little as only one day together.

George wrote to both his parents and Olivia to give them advance notice of his leave, hoping his letters would arrive before he was home. Because flying back in one of the squadron's planes was not an option because of the weather, George had to hope he could pick up a ferry crossing without too much difficulty. Two days after setting off from Arras, a weary George arrived at his parents' home where, to his delight, Olivia was also there to greet him. She had not yet gone back to university but, having received his letter and knowing he would visit his parents first, she decided that she too would be there when he arrived. Expecting it to take the best part of two days to get home, she made her way to George's parents' house arriving there three hours before George did.

George's parents had not known exactly when to expect George but were well prepared in any case. His mother had stocked up with enough food to last the whole week and his father had topped up his drinks cabinet with a bottle of gin and a bottle of whisky. Much as George tried to stay awake as long as he could his first night home and much as he was thrilled to be with Olivia, he could not overcome the tiredness brought on by his journey home and he retired to bed soon after 9:00 p.m. that evening. Being at his parents' house meant that he and Olivia slept in separate rooms but, even if they had been able to spend the night in the same room, he was not sure Olivia could have kept him awake for long.

George needed to work out when he would have head back to France to be back in time before his leave was over. He could not afford to be late for fear of being denied leave in the future and, on the basis it took him two days to get home, he assumed it would take much the same time to return. This would allow him three nights in England before having to make his way back to Arras. Not surprisingly, his parents wanted him to spend all three nights with them but this would not allow Olivia and him as much time to themselves as they would have liked or to spend a night together. George was torn between, on the one hand, telling his parents he would have to leave home a day earlier than he needed to in order that he could spend a night with Olivia and, on the other hand, spending a third night with them, which would deny him a night alone with Olivia. Much as Olivia tried to persuade him to spend only two nights at home, George did not want to lie to his parents about having to leave earlier than was necessary and, aware that there was a real risk that he might never see them again, felt morally obliged to spend as much time as he could with them. Disappointed as she was with his decision, Olivia accepted it but at least had the consolation of knowing that she too would be able to be with George for the three days he was home on leave.

George's time in England passed all too quickly; the daytime was spent with Olivia as they went on walks together and the evenings at home with his parents. Five days after leaving Arras, George was making his way back there; with the journey back being easier than the journey home, he arrived back in Arras in plenty of time before his leave was over.

The weather conditions had not improved whilst George had been on leave and, as a consequence, the opportunities to fly continued to be limited. It was not until late February that they improved enough for the squadron to resume normal reconnaissance and photographic duties.

Fighting on the ground had reached a stalemate with both sides able to defend their entrenched positions along the front line. In early April, this apparent deadlock was broken as the Allied forces launched an attack in and around Arras at the same time as the French were launching an attack in the Aisne region some seventy-five miles away, in an attempt to draw German forces away from that region. Despite being based in Arras, George's squadron was not called upon to assist the ground forces but their presence so close to the fighting gave them cause to be concerned about their own safety. For the first time, they experienced what it was like having to cope with the noise from the continuous artillery barrage which made sleep difficult and to witness casualty levels they had not witnessed before. The fighting continued for over five weeks and only came to an end when it was clear that the British forces were not going to achieve the breakthrough that had prompted them to launch the attack in the first place. In George's view, very little had been gained but at great cost to human life and he was only thankful that serving with his squadron had not exposed him to the same level of risk; it did worry him though that his brother Edward was, in all likelihood, putting his life at risk and he hoped and prayed that Edward would be one of the survivors.

Although the squadron was not called upon for the Battle of Arras, it was called into action three weeks later at Messines, barely ten miles away. Its responsibilities during the battle were no longer merely reconnaissance and photography but, with the planes now equipped with machine guns and bombs, included dropping bombs on enemy lines and firing at enemy planes. The German air force had also been equipping their aircraft in the same way and no longer could the pilots on either side assume they were out of range from enemy fire. The fighting lasted a week during which George's squadron lost two of their planes and with them, four airmen. No longer was flying necessarily a safer option than fighting in the trenches.

Two weeks after the Battle of Messines, George's squadron was posted back in England, at Sutton's Farm in Hornchurch, only fourteen miles from Central London. Much as those in the squadron hoped a posting back in England would take them away from the fighting, this was not the case. Instead, they were now required to deter attacks from the new German Gotha bombers that had launched a number of bombing attacks on London. If anything, the return to England to defend London against the new German planes was every bit as risky as fighting in France and Belgium.

The return of the squadron had the desired effect of deterring the Germans from further aerial attacks on London and once the attacks ceased, there was no need for George's squadron to be called into service to defend London. The lack of action resulted in them being granted their first leave since the beginning of the year before being recalled back to France.

Despite being back in England and so close to London, George had not been able to see his parents or Olivia until granted his four days' leave. Being so close meant he did not have to spend too much of his leave travelling but, as with his previous leave, he had to plan how best to divide his time between his parents and Olivia without upsetting them. He felt the best compromise was to spend the first night with his parents and the rest of his leave with Olivia, albeit at his parents' home for the second and third nights; he would spend his last night with just Olivia.

His parents updated him on Edward's news; serving with the Fourth Army, Edward had survived the last months of the Battle of the Somme the previous year and was based near Ypres, not far from the aerodrome where George had been stationed before George's posting back to England. The newspapers were reporting on a new offensive which had recently been launched by the Allied forces near Passchendaele and, even though the casualty levels were kept out of the news, George knew that they were likely to be high. He did not share this though with his parents, who would only worry more if they knew.

George had to find somewhere to stay with Olivia for his last night of leave and, with him having to report at Hornchurch the next day and with the aerial bombing attacks on London at an end, he opted for London's Savoy Hotel. His parents were saddened by his decision not to spend his last night with them but were understanding; he wanted to be with Olivia and it was not the same when his parents were there as well.

Over dinner, they talked about the first night they had spent together, at the Randolph Hotel the previous October.

"Was I being presumptuous in booking a room for us last year?" George asked Olivia.

"Of course you were. But that doesn't mean it wasn't welcome. What would you have done if I'd said no."

"I don't know but I was pleased you didn't. I suppose I would've been a bit embarrassed for coming across as too forward but it would not have meant I loved you any less. But I was reasonably confident that a girl who climbs into my bed when I'm staying with her parents was unlikely to say no."

"Did you think any less of me because I did say yes?"

"Of course not. It was what I wanted and, had you said no, I think it would only have been a question of waiting until the moment was right. For me, the moment was right then, as it is now."

"The moment was right for me as well and I can't wait for us to finish our meal now and enjoy our time together as we did before. And, for that reason, you're not allowed a glass of port after dinner."

After dinner, George and Olivia retired to their hotel room knowing that it could be the last time they would be together for many months. As they lay next to each other in bed, George started kissing Olivia passionately, first on her lips and then her neck and her back. Eventually she turned to him and told him that she wanted him to make love to her.

"I so want to make love to you as well but shouldn't we wait until we are married?" George responded.

"I know we should but I worry so much that you may not come back from the War and, were that to happen, I would always regret that I would never have shared with you something I want to share only with you."

"Are you sure you won't have any regrets?"

"Completely. I'm not sure what it will be like but whatever it is like, it'll be better than having to live knowing that it never happened."

Their love-making for the first time was more memorable for the experience than the pleasure but when they made love for the second time, the ice had been broken and both found it more pleasurable than the first time. They had not taken much precaution to avoid Olivia becoming pregnant but Olivia told George that this did not bother her; as she explained, if she did become pregnant, she would always have something of him if he did not return from the War and, if he did return from the War, they would get married.

Later that morning, they went their separate ways, with George heading back to Hornchurch and Olivia to her parents' home, to take up, having now graduated, the job she had been offered at the Graylingwall War Hospital in Chichester, a job she had applied for so that she could do her bit for the war effort. Before the day was out, George was back in France. His squadron was now based at Sainte Marie Cappel in northern France, not far from the English Channel and only a little over ten miles away from its previous air base at Le Gorgue.

The squadron spent no more than four weeks at its new base before being relocated to Izel le Hameau, ten miles to the west of Arras. On their return to France, waiting for them were some new planes, single-seater Sopwith Pups. The new aircraft had already proved its superiority over those being flown by the enemy and, even though every pilot in George's squadron was only too aware that the enemy aircraft were also now equipped with machine guns, it was some comfort to know that they were likely to come off better than the enemy in any scrap.

No later than two months after first flying the Pups, George's squadron was equipped with the most recently developed Sopwith plane, the Sopwith Camel. The Camel was fitted with two machine guns which were synchronised to fire through the plane's propellers and with up to four bombs for dropping. At first the new aircraft proved difficult to handle but once the pilots overcame these difficulties, they acknowledged and appreciated that they were more manoeuvrable than the Pups and considerably more so than the Nieuport planes in which they had learned to fly.

Although winter was approaching and, with it, the prospect of a let-up in the fighting, the training exercises undertaken by George's squadron were no less intense, the reason for which was explained to them in the third week of November; the Allied forces were planning to attack the town of Cambrai, an important base for supplies to the Germans' Hindenburg Line. The attack would involve the extensive use of tanks for the first time and would be supported by George's squadron whose role was to drop bombs on German positions.

The battle commenced on 20th November and George, along with eight others from his squadron, took off early in the morning heading towards Cambrai, some twenty-five miles to the east. Their instructions were to drop their bombs as close to the Hindenburg Line as they could and only use their machine guns to defend themselves against any aerial attack. The nine pilots flew their planes in groups of three, with each group assigned a different section of the Hindenburg Line to target. In order to improve their chances of hitting their targets, the pilots were instructed to fly as low as possible; although George and the other two pilots flying beside him managed to get close to their target without coming under attack, they came under heavy fire from the German artillery forces on the ground once they were in a position to drop their bombs. The enemy fire did not deter George and his colleagues from their mission and, although George managed to avoid being hit, Harry, flying on George's starboard side, was less fortunate. Before any of them could offload their bombs, Harry's plane was hit and, with the bombs still on board, the ensuing explosion destroyed Harry's plane and could easily have taken George's plane out as well; George was only too aware that it was a matter of luck rather than judgement that resulted in Harry rather than himself being hit. Less than a minute after losing Harry, George and Frank, who was flying on George's port side, reached their respective targets and dropped their bombs; as soon as the bombs had been dropped, the pilots headed back to their base at Izel le Hameau. On the flight back, they flew low enough to see the Allied forces' slow-moving tanks beneath them heading towards Cambrai. Despite looking cumbersome, they also looked intimidating and fearsome and George was grateful they were part of the Allied forces' armoury rather than the enemy's.

Significant advances were made by the Allied forces on the first day of the battle but, after calling up reinforcements, the German army regained much of the lost ground. On the third day of the battle, George was called into action again, his plane having been reloaded with bombs. As had been the case two days earlier, he set off in a group of three, this time alongside Frank and Bobby, who had joined the squadron six months earlier. The weather was not ideal for flying but the cloudy skies would provide some cover if they needed it. The German ground forces were ready for them as they approached but the three British pilots reached their targets without being hit. As they dropped their bombs, out of the clouds appeared six German planes heading straight towards them. Outnumbered, they knew their best chance of survival was to separate and draw the enemy planes off in different directions and, as Frank steered his plane off in a northerly direction and Bobby in a southerly one, George headed east, in the opposite direction to his air base and over German occupied territory. The plan to draw the enemy planes off in different directions worked in part as only one of the German planes pursued Bobby but Frank still had two of the Germans on his tail and George three. Although the clouds provided George with some cover, he knew that the German pilots would still follow him and, with three against one, the odds were not in his favour but, with his plane being superior to the planes being flown by his pursuers, there was a fair chance he would lose them. Although it seemed much longer, less than five minutes after separating from Frank and Bobby, George lost sight of the Germans following him and thought it safe enough to change direction and head back west to base. Although there was no sign of the three planes that had been following him, within a minute after heading back he was confronted by two of the other German planes flying straight at him. George assumed that they were the same two that had followed Frank but he had no idea whether Frank had managed to evade them or whether Frank's plane had been shot down; either way it took George no time to work out for himself that he could have as many as five enemy planes closing in on him, with two straight ahead of him and possibly three still behind him. He knew that, were he to turn and head back eastwards, there was a greater risk of coming across the three planes he had lost, so he had to choose between heading off northwards or southwards. George chose northwards to avoid the possibility of coming across the plane that had been on Bobby's tail and, assuming Bobby had not been shot down, to avoid him being drawn back into the aerial battle.

Evading his two new followers was proving more challenging than the first three and, although he was able to fire at them, he could only fire at one of them at a time, leaving the other in a position to fire at him without being fired at. George's flying skills were tested to the full as he outwitted the two chasing him but the appearance of a third enemy plane tipped the balance; he was running low on ammunition and fuel, to such an extent that he was no longer sure he had enough fuel to get back to his own base. This became a certainty when machine gun fire hit his fuel tank; he could see from his fuel tank gauge that his time in the air was running out and that before long he would have no choice but to bring the plane down, always assuming he avoided being shot down first. With the Germans still firing at him, George needed to find an aerodrome to land on, even if it was a German one; a crash landing elsewhere was an option but as he was flying over enemy territory, his chances of avoiding capture were at best minimal and his best chance of survival would be to land the plane safely and then sabotage it.

George assumed he would be able to land the plane safely. Knowing the Germans had an air base at Charleroi in Belgium some forty miles behind the Hindenburg Line, George headed in that direction. As he approached the aerodrome at Charleroi still being fired at, he felt a sudden sharp pain in his left arm. He had been hit just above the elbow causing him to let go of the joystick with his injured arm. Handling the plane with two hands on the joystick was difficult enough but with one hand it was almost impossible. George had to get the plane down as quickly as he could as his wound was causing him to lose his strength.

He picked out the runway at the aerodrome from just under half a mile away and, as he approached it, his plane stalled. With his angle of descent, what was left of his fuel was not getting through to the engine and only after levelling out did the engine re-engage. His engine stalled twice more before he reached the runway. George landed the plane heavily and, as the nose of the Camel dipped in front of him, George was unable to hold the plane in a straight line. The plane veered towards the trees to the left of the runway; unable to bring the plane to a halt, George prepared himself for the inevitable crash into the trees. On hitting the trees the plane came to an immediate halt and, although George foresaw this happening, he could not prevent himself being thrown forward into the control panel or his left ankle being crushed, causing him to lose consciousness. The plane caught fire less than a minute after crashing and seconds later the engine exploded.

On his return to Izel le Hameau, Bobby provided his superiors with his version of what had happened, as neither George nor Frank had made it back. Bobby explained that there was not much to tell as, once the enemy planes appeared, he, George and Frank had headed off in different directions and that was the last he saw of either of them. He informed his superiors that, as far as he knew, three of the enemy aircraft had followed George and two had followed Frank and that they were both being pursued the other side of the Hindenburg Line, acknowledging that, as neither of them had returned to base, there was every chance that they had been shot down, even though he had not seen it.

Two days after Bobby had spoken to his superiors, rumours reached the squadron that troops on the ground had witnessed a dogfight involving three enemy aircraft and a British plane, which ended when the British plane was hit and smoke seen pouring from its engine; although no-one witnessed the plane crashing, the troops could see that a crash was inevitable and that it was most unlikely the pilot would survive. Following this report, the squadron assumed that it was George's plane that had been hit as Bobby had reported that there had been three of the enemy aircraft in pursuit; they were not to know that, after losing Bobby, his pursuer joined up with the two pilots following Frank.

Not wanting to spoil Christmas for George's family, George's squadron leader waited until after Christmas before informing the family that George was missing, hopeful that in the meantime there might be some good news about George's whereabouts. No such news was forthcoming.

Part 3

1918

As was her wont, on arrival for work at the hospital Olivia would check the list of new admissions, more to find out how many more patients she would have to attend to than for any other reason; one morning in January as she arrived at work, she recognised a name on the admissions list. Wanting to know more about the new patient, she located the matron on the patient's ward.

"Matron, I noticed this morning a patient called Edward Hart has been admitted to hospital. I know an Edward Hart and I'm anxious to know if he's the Edward Hart I know."

"Olivia, if you'd like to see for yourself, he's in the end bed on the right hand side at the far end of the ward."

Olivia walked to the far end of the ward where she saw in the bed allocated to Edward Hart a man sleeping with a bandage over one of his eyes. Not wanting to disturb him, she tip-toed closer to the bed, close enough to see the patient was indeed George's brother.

Making her way back to the matron, Olivia asked why he had been admitted.

"He's recovering from the effects of a mustard gas attack."

"Is he expected to live?"

"He's one of the luckier ones. A number of his comrades were fatally wounded in the attack. Having survived as long as he has, he's over the worst but he has suffered quite extensive internal and external bleeding and his sight has been affected."

"When will I be able to speak to him?"

"All in good time. He's still under heavy medication but, as soon as he's awake again, we'll call you."

"Thank you Matron."

Later that afternoon, Olivia was told that she could see Edward and, as she made her way to him, wondered how he would react to hearing that he was about to become an uncle. Anxious as she was to find out if Edward had any news of George, she knew that she would first have to enquire how Edward was feeling.

"Not too good but better than I have been" came the reply from Edward.

"D'you want to tell me what happened?"

"I don't recall very much other than we were hit by a mortar attack; the next thing I knew I was in a casualty clearing station."

"Do your parents know you're here?"

"I don't know; I haven't been able to tell them but maybe someone else has. Tell me though Olivia, what are you doing here?"

"After graduating last summer, I applied for a job here as I wanted to help the war effort and I've been working here ever since. As you can probably tell from my shape, I'm not going to be working here much longer as I'll soon be giving birth to your nephew or niece."

"Does George know you are pregnant?"

"I don't know. I only discovered I was pregnant in October and, although I've written to tell him, I haven't heard a word back. Have you heard any news of him?"

"The last I heard was he had been posted back to France in August but I haven't heard anything since then."

Before leaving Edward to let him rest, she told him that she would write to his parents to let them know he was at the hospital and when they could visit him. She hoped too that she could meet up with them not only to find out if they had any news about George but also to tell them that they were about to become grandparents.

That evening, Olivia wrote to George's parents, Albert and Alice, telling them that Edward was at the hospital where she was working; she explained that he was recovering from injuries he had sustained but was on the mend and was able to receive visitors, so she hoped that they would be able to visit him soon. She could not avoid mentioning George in her letter and enquired if they had any news; and as she had already told Edward she was expecting George's child, she told them as well, hoping that they would be excited at the prospect of becoming grandparents.

The letter arrived three days later. Albert read out the letter to Alice and relieved as they were to hear about Edward, the news of Olivia's pregnancy caused them some consternation; unbeknown to Olivia, Albert and Alice had only recently been visited by a representative of George's squadron informing them that, following action in which George had taken part during the Battle of Cambrai, George was missing, presumed dead. Albert and Alice would have to pass on this tragic news to Olivia at some stage but the news of her pregnancy left them in two minds; should they tell her before the baby was born knowing it could affect the pregnancy or should they wait until after the birth? They discussed whether to tell Olivia's parents and leave it to them to pass on the news but felt that they owed it to Olivia to tell her.

Albert and Alice visited the hospital the following weekend. They made their way to Chichester by train and, as no taxis were available to transport them to the hospital, walked the last two miles to the hospital; fortunately, the weather was relatively benign for the time of year, allowing them to arrive at the hospital in dry clothes, even if slightly out of breath. Their first priority was to see Edward and, after waiting no more than ten minutes in the general reception area, one of the nurses introduced herself and asked them to follow her. When they arrived at his bed, Edward was sitting up waiting for them; having passed on their way to Edward a number of other patients covered in bandages, it came as no real surprise to them to see Edward also with bandages over one of his eyes but it was still unsettling for them. They spent an hour with him and, after hearing the ordeal he had been through, more than anything they were relieved he was still in one piece. During their hour together, they broke the news they had received about George to Edward; he took the news somewhat philosophically, because his own war experiences had prepared him better for such an eventuality, but Albert and Alice knew that it would hit him harder once he had time to reflect upon it.

Back in the reception area, they asked if Olivia was on duty and, if so, if she was free to spend a few minutes with them; the receptionist confirmed that Olivia was on duty and would be free to see them in about twenty minutes' time. Waiting to pass on unwelcome news about George was not easy but Albert and Alice had no choice; eventually they could see Olivia walking towards them and that she was well into her pregnancy. Pleased as they were to see each other, Albert did not want to put off breaking the news about George but was not sure when would be the right moment; so worried was he about telling her, it had not registered with him that she was bound to ask if there was any news of George. It did not take long for Olivia to broach the subject.

"Mr and Mrs Hart, is there any news of George? I haven't heard a word from him for well over three months now."

Albert spoke. "Olivia, we fear it's not good news. We've been told that, towards the end of November, he was taking part in an aerial attack behind enemy lines. There is no record of him having been captured alive and he has been reported as "missing presumed dead" but there is no evidence of this. We have to hope for the best."

Olivia did not speak at first, keeping her thoughts to herself. After a while, she replied as if talking to herself.

"I always feared this might happen. I know they tell you someone is "missing, presumed dead" because they don't have any proof of death and probably never will have but once they are missing the chances are they are dead."

Olivia retreated into her own thoughts again before asking if Edward was aware. Albert told her that they had told him earlier that day.

Olivia then spoke again. "I know you must be feeling this loss as much as anyone but is there any way we can find out if he was captured?"

"Olivia, the news was given to us by a member of George's squadron. We were told that, during the battle he was taking part in, troops on the ground witnessed a British plane having been hit by enemy fire and that smoke had been seen pouring from one of the engines. We were also told that only one of the British pilots returned to base and, although a third British pilot was involved in the battle and had not returned to base, by all accounts it seems most likely that the plane which was hit was George's."

"Is there anything you can do to find out if he was captured?"

"We can obviously ask if there's any more news but hopefully they would let us know without having to be asked. We'll ask though as it can't do any harm and we'll let you know if we hear anything."

That evening, Olivia told her parents the news about George. When she had told them about her pregnancy, they had been much more open-minded than she had expected; they had been confident that she and George would marry but, with George dead, they were concerned for her and her unborn child; with the number of war dead increasing, the number of eligible bachelors was falling every day and what chance would an unmarried mother have in finding a man to support her and her child when they could choose from so many without children? However, they did not want to trouble her with their concerns as they were only too aware of how she must be feeling.

For Olivia, her only concern was the loss of George; it was not a loss she could share with her parents as, much as they liked him, he would never mean the same to them as he did to her. As far as she was concerned, it was not them having to deal with the pain and suffering she was enduring and, even if she told how she was felt, they would not really understand. For the best part of two weeks, Olivia hardly spoke to anyone, consumed by her loss. Her colleagues at work left her alone but one afternoon the head nurse at work summonsed her. She told Olivia that everyone felt for her and that, if there was anything anyone could do to help her, they would. Olivia took on board what had been said to her but told the head nurse that it was not something she could share because it was so personal.

"Olivia, you know that many people working here, whether they be patients or members of staff, have had to cope with the loss of someone close to them; most of them have lost close ones because of this dreadful war. I understand that everyone copes with such losses in their own way. In your case, your loss is every bit as great a loss as everyone else's but, in your case, there is someone who you may not recognise is also having to share the same loss as you. Have you thought of talking to Edward who'll not only understand better than anyone how you're feeling but will also benefit from sharing his loss?"

"No, I haven't thought about it. I'll think about it though."

Olivia appreciated that sharing her loss with Edward would do neither of them any harm but she was uncertain what she should say to Edward. She knew she would have to take the initiative but did not know how to raise the subject with him. After a couple of days worrying what she should say, she sought her mother's advice; her mother told her to imagine what she would expect Edward to say to her, if it was Edward trying to console her rather than the other way round.

Three days later, she plucked up the courage to speak to Edward.

"Edward, in my grief, I feel I've been rather selfish and not given enough thought to the suffering of others. Because of this, I've ignored you and what you must be feeling about George. I hope therefore that we can help each other deal with a loss which, even if it affects us differently, is equally painful for both of us."

Edward gave himself time to think how best to respond; he knew his reaction to the loss of George was different to Olivia's.

"Olivia, I'm of course feeling the loss of George greatly; growing up, he was always there for me and I always looked to him for support. I'm perhaps more resigned to it than you because of what I've witnessed. Of course, I prayed that George and I would come through the War unscathed but I knew that there was every chance that one of us, if not both of us, wouldn't. His loss may not come as much of a shock to me as to you but that does not mean I don't feel it; I do but, as you rightly say, I feel it in a different way to you."

"Does that mean you don't think we can help each other?"

"Of course not. I think we just need to understand that, how ever much we want to try and help each other, we may not always be able to because we don't understand what the other is feeling. Nonetheless I'll always be here for you if you need me."

Even though Edward's willingness to share their grief came across to her somewhat half-heartedly, she was grateful for these words. She promised Edward that she would make more of an effort to visit and talk to him when she was off duty.

Olivia kept to her word and visited Edward at every available opportunity, with both of them looking forward to their time together and recognising that, in their grieving, they benefited from each other's company. It was only when Olivia stopped working at the hospital at the end of the eighth month of her pregnancy that her visits came to a stop but before taking her leave, she promised to let Edward know as soon as she could whether he had a nephew or a niece.

Olivia spent the last month of her pregnancy at home, tended to by her mother and to a lesser extent, by her sisters. In early April, she gave birth to a girl. Never having experienced pain like it before, she took some convincing by the midwife that the birth had been relatively straightforward but there were no complications for her to have to worry about, other than the one she was only too aware of - that the baby's father was presumed dead.

She spent the next two weeks at home, resting whenever her baby allowed it. Much as she was overjoyed with its arrival, it reminded her of how much she was missing George. Not having him around to see his own child, not having him there to choose a name together and not having him there to share her joy not only brought her great sadness but also convinced her even more that he would never be returning from the War.

When Olivia was fit enough, she arranged to visit the hospital where she had worked, not just to see her former colleagues but also Edward. Her colleagues were thrilled to hear her news but Edward had been discharged and was now recuperating at home with his parents. Although she was disappointed not to see him, she was delighted to hear that his health had improved as it would allow her to visit him and his parents, whom she was sure would be longing to meet their first grandchild. She wrote to them to tell them her news and asked when would be convenient to visit them.

On being presented with their first grandchild George's parents were as doting and proud as Olivia's parents had been and, within only minutes of seeing Jill for the first time, Alice commented that she could see a lot of George in her and how she looked like George at that age. Not having heard any more news about George since Olivia had last seen his parents over three months ago, Alice's comments prompted Olivia to ask about him. Albert told her that, following his and his wife's visit to the hospital, he had contacted George's squadron but there was no more news about him.

This brought Albert on to the subject of money.

"Olivia, with George's whereabouts unknown, we want you to know that we'll provide you with whatever financial support you feel you need for Jill. We feel it's our duty to ensure that you and Jill do not suffer as a consequence of whatever has happened to him."

"Mr Hart, that's very kind of you. I've not given it any thought as I'm currently being well looked after at home."

"We wouldn't want you to think you have to go back to work in order to give Jill the upbringing she would've had if George had returned and we'll help if need be."

"Neither would I want to take advantage of such a generous offer. I clearly need to give some thought to my and Jill's future but, as things are at present, I'm learning to adjust to motherhood, taking one step at a time. But I can't thank you enough for your kind offer."

Later in the day, Edward returned home; his wounds had led to him being discharged from his regiment and he now had a desk job at the War Office. As well as providing him with an income, he hoped it would also allow him access to records which would reveal if there was any news of George. To date though, there was nothing new to report.

Edward had missed Olivia and their time together when he had been in hospital and was keen to catch up as well as to being introduced to his niece. Olivia was pleased to see him. Since she had stopped working at the hospital, the only men she had had contact with were her father and the boys at her father's school and she longed to spend some time in the company of a man more her own age. Edward's mannerisms reminded her of George and, although that saddened her in some ways, it also brought back happy memories.

Before she left for home the next day, Edward told her that he was planning to pay a visit to the hospital in Chichester that had cared for him and asked if he might call in on her while he was in the area. She told Edward that she was sure her parents would be willing to provide him with a bed for the night.

Once back with her parents, Olivia mentioned the offer of financial support from George's father. Her father was relieved that she had brought the subject up because he knew that before too long they would need to discuss her longer term plans.

"It's very considerate of Mr Hart to offer to help you financially", he said. "Of course, if you need any financial support, your mother and I can also help. I'm sure we can find work for you at my school if that's what you want – and your mother can look after Jill whilst you're out. But you need to be thinking about your own welfare as well. With no news of George, is being an unmarried mother in your best interests?"

"I have to believe George will come back and, when he does, we shall marry. I'm only too aware that Jill has been born out of wedlock but, outside of our families, no one need know that."

"That may be the case if George does return but what if he doesn't? You can't just change your name to his and pretend you were married. You'll still be a Phillips and have to live with the stigma of having an illegitimate child. That doesn't worry your mother or me but others will have a different, less enlightened view about it. I just don't think you should pin all your hopes on George coming back. There's been no news of him for close on six months now and there's little sign of the War coming to an end soon. And, even if he's alive, can you be sure that the War won't have changed him?"

"I'll only ever know the answer to that if and when he returns but, as I've said, I have to believe he will one day. If the War has changed him that's something I'll have to deal with at the time."

"You might have to wait a long time and you have to think about Jill as well. It won't be long before she needs a father figure in her life."

"Father, if George does return, Jill will have a father figure and if he doesn't, Jill will be in the same position as many others who've already lost or will lose their fathers in this War."

"The fact that other families may be in the same position will be of no benefit to Jill. Let's not talk about it anymore now but do bear in mind what I've said."

Over the following days Olivia did indeed take on board what her father had said but it only made her more aware of the terrible dilemma she faced. Could she allow her heart which made her believe George would return to win over her head, which reasoned that his return was unlikely? The more she thought about it the more she acknowledged that he might not return. However, now was not the time for facing up to it – that would have to wait until she knew for certain.

Three weeks after staying with George's parents, Olivia received a letter from Edward informing her that he was planning to visit the hospital in Chichester within the next fortnight and asking if her offer of a bed for the night at her parents' house was still open. Olivia replied by return informing him that she would be delighted to see him again if he had the time to call in on her and that there would be a bed for him if he wished to stay the night.

Edward found his own way to the Phillips' home after his visit to the hospital. He had not met Olivia's parents before or her sisters but he was made to feel very welcome in their home. As always when Olivia saw Edward, she wanted to know if there was any news of George; Edward told her that he had made enquiries at the War Office but there was nothing new to report. He explained that the War Office would not expect to hear whether or not George was being held as a prisoner-of-war and George's squadron had not come up with anything new.

That there was no new news left Olivia with mixed feelings. On the one hand, being told there was nothing new to report made her worry that George might be dead but on the other hand it was not the news she was most dreading and therefore gave her something to hope for.

The following morning Olivia accompanied Edward to the station to catch his train. On their way there Edward repeated the offer which his parents had made to provide financial support and also told her that he too was willing to help if he could as he too wanted to ensure Jill was well looked after. Olivia was not sure what he had in mind but thanked him and promised that she and Jill would keep in regular touch with George's family.

Olivia paid her second visit with Jill to see George's parents in the last week of July. By then, Jill was coming up to four months old and starting to develop her own personality. As with the time they first saw Jill, they could see a lot of George in her looks in much the same way Olivia's parents could see a lot of Olivia in Jill. It did not take Olivia long before asking if there was any more information about George. Again the response was there was nothing new to report.

Edward joined them in the evening after work and, although that there was still no news about George, Olivia was keen to hear from Edward how the war effort was progressing; for her own peace of mind, Olivia wanted to have some idea how long she might have to wait before George would be returning, assuming of course he was still alive. Edward explained to her that, although the Americans had joined the War some fifteen months earlier, it had not been enough to bring a decisive end to the War. It had allowed the Allied Forces to strengthen their defences but had had little impact on breaking down the German defences, which had been strengthened by the withdrawal of the Russians from the War, allowing German troops on the Eastern Front fighting the Russians to be redeployed on the Western Front to fight the Allied troops. Edward added that the German Spring Offensive which had started in March had come to an end only days earlier without the Germans making a decisive breakthrough but, with each side in the conflict in much the same position as it had been in before the Spring Offensive had been launched, it was difficult to see how the deadlock would be broken; Edward's view, which he shared with his parents and Olivia, was that, if neither side was able to gain any ground after four months of fierce fighting, neither side had enough firepower to bring the War to an end in the foreseeable future and therefore, in his opinion, the War had months, if not years, still to run. When asked by Olivia if this view was shared by his colleagues at the War Office, Edward told her that he thought it was but the propaganda war machine almost certainly gave the public another impression.

Edward had the following day off work, it being a Saturday and after breakfast he and Olivia, along with Jill in her pram, went for a long walk along the Thames towpath. They joined the path half a mile up river from Putney and walked the route of the Boat Race all the way to Barnes Bridge before heading back. Away from his parents, Edward was keen to explain to Olivia what he had meant when they had last seen each other.

"Olivia, I know when we last saw each other I offered to help you out if that's what you wanted. I hope it won't embarrass you but I want to explain to you what I meant by this and why I said it. As you know, I joined the Army straight after leaving school; I have no sisters and was at a boys' boarding school so the only young woman I know is you. Of course I've met other young women, such as when I was in hospital but I've never really known a woman I can call a friend, other than you. And, not just as a friend but also because of the family connection, I want to help you if, because of your own situation, you need any help. As I see it, your situation is that you're an unmarried mother and, much as I hate to believe it, the father of your child has been killed in the War. With the loss of so many men of our generation, there'll be plenty of women who'll end up as spinsters or widows because there won't be enough men for them all. In your case, having a child won't make it any easier or, just as importantly, for someone to play the role of father to Jill."

Olivia interrupted him before he could say any more. "Edward, I'm not sure where this is leading. I of course can't deny that I'm an unmarried mother but to say the father of my child, your own brother, has been killed has not yet been proven. It's only presumed because it is convenient for it to be presumed but I 've not given up hope."

"Olivia, I admire you enormously for that and I wish I could feel the same. But with witnesses reporting a plane being shot down in a battle in which he was engaged and not a word from or about him since, it's only being realistic to presume he's dead. Perhaps it's just that I'm more prepared to accept his fate than you are."

"Anyway, what was it you were going to say before I interrupted you?"

"It's just that our situation, assuming George doesn't return, is one where you may not find it easy to find a husband who can be a father to Jill and, with the injuries I've sustained, I may not find it that easy to find a wife or indeed be able to have my own children. A solution to this could be ...".

Olivia interrupted him again before he could finish.

"Edward, are you suggesting that the two of us get married?"

"Not exactly; what I'm suggesting is that, if you wanted to find a husband who could act as a father to Jill, I'd be willing to fill that role. You wouldn't find anyone who's closer to George in terms of personality and, as Jill is my niece, I'd look after her as if she were my own."

Realising that he was being earnest, Olivia did not take offence but instead tried to laugh it off.

"Edward, you're not being serious, are you?"

"Olivia, I'm sorry if I've offended you. I haven't intended to. It was just something that I thought might be of mutual convenience to both of us but, if it's of no interest, let's pretend we never had this conversation. But, if it is of interest to you, then yes, I am being serious."

"Edward, I haven't taken offence and perhaps I should be flattered. Such a proposal, albeit not a formal one, is totally unexpected. But it's not one I can entertain whilst I have some hope in George returning."

"Would your view be any different if you knew George wouldn't be returning?"

"I don't know; I suppose I can only answer that if and when I know he's not returning."

"It's now coming up to nine months since there's been any word from George. I'm going to make another effort to see if anyone can provide any information about what might have happened to him. One of the pilots in George's squadron who was in the aerial battle with George survived the battle and I'll see if I can meet him, assuming he's still alive. I'll let you know what he says. Of course, I hope that he'll say that George survived but, if he were to confirm that he didn't, I'll tell you and ask you to bear in mind what I've said."

"Edward, I know you well enough to know that what you've suggested is with the best intentions. But you must understand that I can't plan anything for the future other than one with George whilst I still believe there is a possibility he will return."

No more was said on the subject. Olivia and Jill spent one more night with the Hart family before they made their way home to her parents. Olivia told her parents about the conversation she and Edward had had and, like Olivia, they did not know what to make of it at first but, after allowing herself a few moments to think about it, Olivia's mother spoke.

"Olivia darling, he must obviously be very fond of you. He surely wouldn't have suggested offering himself for marriage otherwise."

"Mother, that's all very well but I don't love him. I like him and am fond of him too but that's not enough to make me want to marry him."

"Of course your father and I understand that and we'd never want you to feel under any pressure to marry against your will. I'm sure Edward's intentions were entirely honourable even if somewhat misguided."

Olivia's father joined in the discussion. "Olivia, at least you have a suitor and in these difficult times, there'll be many a young lady who'll have no suitors simply because there aren't going to be enough young men to go round. Much as Edward's suggestion may not be of interest to you, there may come a time when you'll be grateful for it."

"Father, now is not the time for me to be grateful for it, however flattering it is."

The tone of Olivia's response was enough to make her parents realise that enough had been said for the time being.

As he had promised to Olivia before she returned home, Edward contacted George's squadron. It was still based in France which meant Edward would not be able to meet any members of the squadron unless they were on leave. He sent a communication to the squadron in France informing them that he was keen to speak to the pilot called Bobby who had flown with George in the battle of Cambrai and also see a copy of the squadron's official account of the battle. Edward received a reply ten days later informing him that, since the battle of Cambrai, Bobby had been killed in action; with regard to the request to see the official account of the battle, Edward was informed that the squadron could not make a copy of the official account available but could provide details of what was recorded in the account. On the assumption Edward would want to know such details, the squadron informed Edward that they would be sending them to him at the War Office. Four days later, Edward received a letter from the squadron's new commander; in the letter, the commander told Edward that he had seen the official record and that, although it was not conclusive because of the lack of eye –witness accounts, the most likely scenario was that George's plane had been shot down. The commander explained that the squadron had drawn this conclusion because one of the other pilots in the battle had reported seeing three enemy aircraft in pursuit of George and because ground forces had seen an Allied aircraft shot down when being pursued by three enemy aircraft; the lack of any news about George since led them to believe he had been lost in action. The commander finished the letter by saying that George was a first-class pilot who had served the squadron and his country with great distinction and that his sympathies were with George's family.

On receiving the letter, Edward wrote to Olivia and, as well as passing on what he had been told, put forward more forcibly his informal proposal to support her and Jill.

The letter arrived two days later. After reading it to herself, Olivia sat in silence until her mother asked her if she was alright. Unsure how to answer, Olivia read the letter out to her mother.

"My dear Olivia,

I trust you are keeping in good health and that my darling niece Jill is too.

When we last met, I promised that I would make further enquiries about George. The commander of George's squadron has responded to my enquiries and I regret that there is nothing new or positive to report. Based on the eye-witness accounts and the fact that there has been no news of George, the squadron has drawn the inevitable conclusion that George was killed in action; furthermore, the one pilot who flew alongside George during the battle and had returned to base has since been killed. The commander was kind enough to comment that George had served his squadron and indeed his country with great distinction.

I have also reported this to my parents and they, like me, are resigned to the fact that George was killed in action.

In view of this, the proposal I put to you when we were walking together beside the Thames remains open. I believe there are good reasons why you should take it seriously. First, because of the family connection, I am better placed than any other man to care for and look after Jill. Secondly, even though George and I are not the same, there is no one whose character and personality are closer to his than mine and if, as I know is the case, you loved George, I would hope that in time you would learn to love me. And lastly, and just as importantly, this dreadful war has caused both of us suffering which we have not chosen for ourselves and which we will never forget; but I think sharing our suffering and loss will be better for both of us than trying to cope with it alone.

It is for these reasons that I would like you to consider my proposal that we be married.

I do not expect an immediate reply but ask that you to give it serious thought before replying. I am obviously prepared to wait for your answer but hope that I do not have to wait too long.

My parents send you and Jill their love and your parents their best wishes, as do I.

With much affection,
Edward"

"Well, what do you make of all that?" asked her mother.

"I like Edward but that's all. He's a good man and I know he means well and I don't want to hurt his feelings but it just does not seem right."

"I understand how you feel but not everything in this world is right; it's not right that George isn't here with you and Jill but there's nothing we can do about that. We have to accept where fate may lead us and adapt accordingly."

"Mother, are you saying you think I should accept Edward's proposal?"

"Darling, I'm not saying that at all. What I'm saying is that, in deciding whether or not to accept it, you need to consider whether, on balance, your life will be more fulfilled accepting his proposal than declining it. Of course, you'll never know the answer to this once you have made your decision; only time will tell whether or not you regret the decision you make but you do at least have a choice. And, in making your choice, you need to consider whether or not Jill's life will be the better for you accepting Edward's proposal."

"I have thought about that and I can see that, as far as Jill is concerned, it is better that she has a father figure and that her father figure is Edward rather than someone else unconnected to the family but, as her uncle, I'd hope Edward will always be there for her anyway."

"I'm sure he will but it would not be the same if there was someone else around."

"Mother, what would you do if you were in my position?"

"It's difficult for me to answer that because I'm not suffering from George's absence in the same way emotionally as you. But assuming you want to be married and have someone who can help you bring up Jill and assuming George will not be returning from the War, I would consider whether being married to Edward, who is so obviously in love with you even if you're not in love with him, is a better option than waiting to see if there's someone else out there you'd prefer to be married to. If you wait, there won't necessarily be that many to choose from and, in the case of a good number of those you would be able to choose from, they'll be unsuitable anyway. As you'll have seen for yourself when working at the hospital, many of those who do return from the War are affected by it one way or another whether it be physically or mentally and those of the right age who have not gone to war will probably be unsuitable for the same reasons they never went to war in the first place. I can't imagine you'd want to marry a conscientious objector or someone who wasn't fit enough to fight for his country."

"Mother, I feel as though you're saying I should accept Edward's proposal."

"No, I'm not saying that. What I'm saying is only you can make the decision but, in making it, you must think what is best for you and the likely consequences of the choices open to you."

Olivia took a fortnight to make up her mind. She did not want to spend the rest of her life as a widow and recognised that this was a distinct possibility, being an unmarried mother. Much as she was confident that, given enough time to overcome the loss of George, she would be able to find another man she could fall in love with, she was less confident such a man would fall in love with her, with her illegitimate child. Going over the same question time and time again she felt cornered. Would she prefer to be married to someone who loved her and would care for her and Jill but whom she did not love or would she prefer to wait and see if someone more suitable, whom she loved, came along but in the knowledge such a man might never come along? The first person she told of her decision was her mother, as if she needed to justify her decision to herself before letting Edward know.

"Mother, I've thought long and hard about whether to accept Edward's proposal. I've taken into account the sound advice you've given me and I've come to the conclusion that as I do not want to spend the rest of my life as an unmarried mother, Edward's proposal may well be the best offer I'm likely to get. I also have to think of Jill and I recognise that Edward is likely to love her and care for her in a way which other men might find more difficult. Much as it's not what I would choose if circumstances were different, I can't change that, so I've decided to accept his proposal."

"Olivia, I think you have made the right decision. And, if I may give you one more piece of advice, now that you've made your mind up, don't ever question yourself whether it was the right decision or not; and you'll only avoid questioning yourself about it if you commit yourself to your marriage whole-heartedly. And, one last word on the subject, if you haven't told Edward yet, don't you think you shouldn't keep him waiting any longer to hear your answer?"

Later that day Olivia wrote to Edward, giving him her answer. She wondered whether their wedding should be postponed until after late November, just over a year since George had disappeared but, having made her decision, she was not one for dragging it out. With Olivia being an unmarried mother, a church wedding was inappropriate even if the church permitted it and instead, on Friday 4th October 1918, they tied the knot at the Chichester Register Office, with Edward's parents and Olivia's parents, sisters and daughter as the only witnesses.

With Edward was still working for the War Office at the time of their marriage, the first weeks of married life were spent with him living with his parents during the week and with Olivia living with her parents in Sussex, where Edward joined them for the weekend. Olivia settled into married life with Edward more easily than she had expected and it was not long before she started to miss him when he was away during the week. A little over five weeks after they married, the War came to an end, leaving Edward with the choice of staying with the War Office or following his father's footsteps into the world of stockbroking; with the latter offering greater financial rewards and better prospects and, with it, the opportunity to rent a home for his new family, Edward started as a junior in his father's office at the beginning of 1919. Within weeks of starting his new job, he and Olivia had found a place to rent in Putney, not far from his parents' home and close enough for Olivia to call upon Edward's mother for help with Jill if ever she needed it.

Part 4

November 1917 – December 1918

George was unconscious for no more than ten seconds after being thrown against the control panel after his crash landing. On regaining consciousness, he knew he had to get away from his plane and that he had little time within which to do so; the pain down his left hand side in the arm and ankle made his escape from the cockpit on to a wing far from straightforward but once on the wing, he lowered himself to the ground allowing him to get away from the plane before it exploded. As he lay on the ground, he noticed he was no longer alone as two Germans approached him pointing guns at him. Unable to lift his left arm and unable to put any weight on his left leg, George did not move other than to put his right arm above his head.

"Don't shoot, don't shoot" he pleaded. "I'm unarmed."

As one of the Germans raised his rifle to fire at George, a third German approached and turning to face his comrade ordered him to lower his gun. George was left in no doubt which of the two of them was the higher ranking.

"Can you not see that this man is wounded? D'you want to be court-martialled for killing an unarmed, injured man?" He then turned to face George.

"Keep your hands to your side or above your head".

"I'm wounded; I can't move my left arm and I can't walk."

"Stay where you are then and don't move."

Seeing that his injuries were serious, the two Germans who had been first to arrive at the scene of the crash went to fetch a stretcher and carried him back to the nearest hangar, where one of the Germans stayed with him. After George had been lying in the hangar for little more than ten minutes, another German appeared and asked George to show him the wounds to his arm and foot. Seeing the injuries, the German knew that something would need to be done immediately to stop the bleeding to his arm. George's ankle was also causing him considerable pain and, although there was little that could be done straightaway, George was offered a crutch but declined it because of the injury to his arm.

Later that day, George was summonsed to a room where an official-looking German officer told him what lay ahead for him. He was now a prisoner-of-war and would be transferred to the Labry Military Hospital in Lorraine at the earliest opportunity; as soon as he was fit enough to be released from the military hospital, the authorities in Berlin would determine which prisoner-of-war camp he would be sent to.

George spent two uncomfortable days and nights at the airdrome before he was transported in an ambulance, along with two injured German soldiers, to the military hospital. The route they took was never far from the Western Front and, as a consequence, the journey was slow as the ambulance transporting them frequently had to give way to supply vehicles heading in the opposite direction. It was not until nightfall that they reached their destination. George spent his first night in a ward with 30 other injured soldiers, all of whom were German. It proved not to be a peaceful night with the medical staff on duty throughout the night tending to patients who required doses of morphine to relieve them of their pains.

The following day George was seen by one of the doctors. With the doctors under instructions to ensure that those being treated were released from hospital at soon as they were fit enough to go, the doctor told George he could expect to be out of the hospital within seven days; he was unable to tell George where he would then be sent but tried to humour him by telling him that they were unlikely to be sending him back to England.

George was looked after well whilst at Labry. The doctors tending to his wounds bore no grudge that they were treating an enemy airman, no doubt thankful that their skills excused them from having to put up with what their patients had had to put up with. To his surprise, George had not broken his ankle during his crash landing but his ankle ligaments were torn badly enough for his ankle to need plastering. More serious was the wound to his left arm; the machine gun fire had gone straight through George's arm causing minimal external bleeding but, whilst passing through his arm, a bullet had damaged the humerus bone just above the elbow. A splint was required to restrict movement of the arm.

With his ankle in plaster and his splinted arm in a sling, George had expected to be in the hospital for seven days, but as there was little more the doctors could do, he was released after only five days into the care of the hospital for wounded prisoners-of-war at Metz, no more than 10 miles away. On arrival at his new hospital, George was told that he would be kept there until the damaged arm had recovered enough for the splint to be removed, after which it was likely that he would be transferred to the camp for prisoners-of-war just outside Metz.

George was just one of four hundred wounded prisoners being cared for at the hospital in Metz, most of whom were French and most of the rest of whom were British. After a restless first night, George was approached the following morning by a fellow Englishman who introduced himself as Captain Douglas Ashby. As the most senior ranking British officer at the hospital, Ashby was keen to know why George was there and to tell George what life was like at the hospital. George explained what had happened to him, following which he was told in no uncertain terms how fortunate he had been. George had been informed by Ashby that only the lucky ones ended up in hospital as many of the

Germans adopted a policy of finishing off the wounded, to spare them any responsibility for having to care for them. George was told that most of the medical staff was friendly enough towards the prisoners but he was also warned that there were a few who cared little for them and George needed to be mindful of them. Later in the day, George was attended to by an Austrian doctor working at the hospital. The doctor told George that he would be detained at the hospital until the injury to the bone in his arm had mended and that that was likely to take up to ten weeks.

At the hospital, George preferred to keep to himself; in light of Ashby's warning about some of his German captors, George took the view that it was better to keep a low profile rather than do anything which might draw himself to their attention; causing trouble for them would, without doubt, cause trouble for himself. As wounded soldiers arrived at the hospital, those already at the hospital were keen to hear news of how the War was progressing but, with little activity on the Western Front over the winter months, the number of new prisoners arriving and news from the Front almost came to a halt.

During George's time at the hospital, prisoners came and went. None were particularly keen to leave as they knew life in the hospital, albeit by no means comfortable, was better than in the prisoner-of-war camps they would be bound for. Christmas too came and went with little cause for celebration amongst the patients. As well as there being little news about how the War was progressing, there was little news from home and, for a large number of the patients, Christmas gave them cause to reflect on how much they were missing their families.

By the end of January, George's wound to his arm had recovered enough for him to be transferred to the prisoner-of-war camp at Strasbourg approximately one hundred miles away. He was transported there by train, along with four others being released from the hospital, in a cattle truck and, on arrival in Strasbourg, they were escorted the final four miles of their journey on foot to their new prison. On arrival at the camp, George was taken to his living quarters, a wooden hut where another fifteen prisoners-of-war were housed. In total there were fifty huts at the camp, housing in excess of seven hundred prisoners, made up mostly of Frenchmen and approximately two hundred British soldiers or airmen; the balance was made up of those from other countries in the British Commonwealth who had volunteered to fight, along with a handful of Belgians and Dutchmen.

It did not take long for George to settle in to routine camp life. Those sharing the hut with him showed him where everything was and explained to him where he needed to be and when – it did not need much explaining as they were in a confined space and there was little to do to fill the time of day. The prisoners were woken at 7:30 each morning and, for those who wanted to attend, a prayer meeting held in the open at 8 o'clock, before breakfast was served an hour later. After breakfast, the prisoners were required to attend a roll-call at 10 o'clock, following which the prisoners' time was their own until lunch at 13:00. Most prisoners used this time to attend classes or lectures put on by other prisoners. After lunch, exercise classes were run and, in order to maintain certain levels of fitness, the prisoners were encouraged to participate. Once a week a game of football was organised and usually those not interested in playing took great pleasure in watching the proceedings.

The guards took little interest in the prisoners provided they behaved in accordance with the camp rules and the prisoners took little interest in the guards other than to enquire on the current state of play on the Western Front. Not surprisingly, the guards told the prisoners that it would not be long before the German Army had defeated the French and British Armies as this was what the guards were being told by their superiors. It did not take long though for prisoners to dismiss such reports as the guards had been passing on the same message for the best part of three years with no end to the War in sight.

As a prisoner, George was allowed to send one letter home every month; each week he wrote to his parents but he had been warned that the Germans could not be relied upon to post the letters; from what he could gather, only a handful of letters were actually posted and, of those that were posted, only a handful ever made it home. George had hoped that, by writing home, he would hear news from his family but the lack of any news from them left him believing he was one of the unlucky ones whose letters never reached their intended destination.

George kept himself busy in the camp. He regularly took part in the organised football matches between teams representing different huts and with so many Frenchmen in the camp, he took the opportunity to improve the basic French he had learnt in school. It was on the football pitch that George first met Henri Latour, who had been taken prisoner by the Germans back in October 1916 during the battle of Verdun. Henri was from a small village in Normandy that George had never heard of and, as he was keen to improve his English in the same way George was keen to improve his French, they spent time together speaking each other's language. It did not take either of them long to reach a level of fluency in the other's language although Henri was never able to master an English accent any more than George was able to master a French one.

One of the many frustrations of being a prisoner was not knowing how long they would kept prisoner and what would happen if and when the War came to an end. This inevitably led to talk about escaping. With the camp being so many miles inside enemy territory, such talk was of little interest to George as he believed the risks involved were too high. News filtered through to the camp in March 1918 that the Russians had given up fighting on the Eastern Front, causing concern amongst the prisoners that this would strengthen the German forces on the Western Front. But with new prisoners arriving at the camp came news of the lack of progress being made by the Germans and the likelihood that the presence of American troops would break the resolve of the Germans before too long.

Further signs that the War was not going Germany's way came over the summer months when the prisoners noticed that there was less food at meal times, not just for the prisoners but for the guards as well. The blockading of the Baltic Sea by the British Navy was having its desired effect, causing food shortages in Germany. The guards were reluctant to be drawn on the causes of the food shortages and the prisoners had little choice but to cope as best they could.

By the end of the summer, the intake of prisoners seemed to slow down but the guards explained that this due to the camp not having the capacity to take any more; the prisoners were not convinced by this because those prisoners who had not been well enough to survive the camp conditions were not being replaced by new arrivals. The lack of new arrivals meant the lack of news, with the prisoners having to rely on such information as the guards were willing to pass on; however, experience told the prisoners that the guards were only passing on what they had been told, much of which was no more than propaganda designed to boost morale and therefore taken by the prisoners with a pinch of salt.

Despite the lack of reliable news reaching the prisoners, rumours were circulating that the Germans had suffered a couple of major setbacks on the Western Front in August and September. Although the majority of guards scoffed at such rumours, the prisoners noticed a change in the guards' demeanour; there was no longer the arrogance that the prisoners felt was so misplaced in guards who had never seen action.

As the summer months wore on, the prisoners found that they were not only having to deal with food shortages but also a flu epidemic; the arrival in Europe of troops from other parts of the world had brought the Spanish flu to the battlefields of Europe and such was the severity of the virus that it was accounting for more deaths than those killed in the fighting. The prisoners and guards at the Strasburg prisoner-of- war camp were not immune from catching the virus and, by the end of the summer of 1918, the death toll amongst prisoners reached double figures. Camp conditions and nutritional deficiencies were such that they hindered the chances of survival and, with another winter about to set in, the prisoners were worried that they might not see it through.

In early November, the camp commander called the most senior British officer, Captain Robert Woollard to his office; the call came somewhat out of the blue as it had been more than three months since he had last received such a summons. The commander explained that he had informed that the War might well be at an end within a matter of days and that, if this was the case, the prisoners should prepare themselves for this. When asked what his source of this information was, the camp commander only responded that his source was a reliable one.

This information was passed on to the prisoners and much as it was welcome, some were unwilling to believe it whilst others worried what would happen to them. They would all want to find their way home but no one knew how they would get there. Four days after their meeting, the commander asked Captain Woollard to report to him again. At this second meeting, the commander reported that earlier that day a meeting had taken place between representatives of the German High Command and the Allied forces at which it had been agreed that hostilities were to cease at 11 o'clock that day. The commander told Captain Woollard that the guards were being released from their camp duties and the prisoners were free to leave; he warned that, although it had been agreed hostilities were at an end, it could take several days before the fighting in some areas stopped. Prisoners making their way home still had to travel at least one hundred kilometres across Alsace and Lorraine, which had been German territory since 1871, before reaching France and the commander advised that prisoners heading home should try and avoid coming across any German soldiers making their way home in the opposite direction in case any were sufficiently embittered to want to take some sort of revenge.

Captain Woollard called a meeting of all British prisoners-of-war at which he passed on the news that the War was officially over. After the cheering had died down, he said that it would take a few days before repatriation plans could be finalised and the prisoners were asked to remain patient whilst such plans were being put together.

George wanted to share his excitement over his imminent release from camp with Henri. They discussed their plans for travelling home and as Paris was en route for Henri's journey home and not out of George's way for his return journey, they agreed to travel to Paris together and, if they felt up to it, enjoy a celebratory evening out whilst there.

Four days after being told that the War was over, George and Henri set off for Paris. By the end of the first day, they had picked up lifts to take them as far as Nancy where they spent the night in the waiting room at the railway station, in the hope that they could board the first westbound train. It was not until late the following morning that the first train heading in the direction of Paris left the station, with George and Henri aboard. Once aboard, they went without food and drink as neither was available on the train, causing them to break their journey and disembark before the day was out. With neither of them having any money, they relied on the good nature of those they met to provide them with sustenance. Despite being no more than forty miles away, numerous unscheduled stops meant it took them four hours to reach St Dizier, where they spent the rest of the day in the hope of finding food.

The residents of St Dizier were more accommodating than those in Nancy, which George and Henri put down to St Dizier, unlike Nancy, being in a part of France which had not occupied by the Germans. The locals were only too keen to ensure the two of them were properly fed and given a comfortable bed for the night, appreciating the sacrifices they had made for their countries and to make France a free country again.

The following day George and Henri were given a lift as far as Vitry, fifteen miles from St Dizier, along with provisions to last them the day. In Vitry, they secured another lift taking them a further twenty miles to Chalons-en-Champagne. They had planned to reach Reims by the evening but it was not until the following morning that they secured a lift that took them there. Once in Reims, they headed for the railway station hoping to catch a train to take them on the final leg of their journey together before going their separate ways.

When they arrived at the railway station they were struck with how busy it was, with numerous troops returning home from the Western Front via Reims; trains were scarce and, once ready to leave, over-crowded. They managed to board a train bound for Paris but it was another two hours after boarding before the train left the station; by the time they had boarded, all available seats were taken and they were left having to find somewhere to sit in the limited corridor space.

By the time the train was pulling into the outskirts of Paris, some three hours after leaving Reims, the colour in Henri's face had paled. When asked by George if he was alright, Henri said that he was feeling a bit feverish and would just want to find a bed for the night once they arrived in Paris. George was determined to help his friend and, after disembarking, told Henri to remain at the station whilst he went in search of a room. George had no joy in finding a hotel room but no more than half a mile away from the railway station, found himself outside the St Louis Hospital. George realised that, as well as being the most likely place to find a bed for Henri, it was also in all likelihood the best place for him. Rather than checking whether or not they would admit Henri, George thought it better to bring Henri to the hospital where his condition could be assessed.

He found Henri where he had left him at Gare de l'Est and told him that, as he had had no success in finding a room for the night, he was taking him to the nearby hospital. On arrival at the hospital, George explained that his friend was returning home from the War and needed a bed for the night as he was not well; being far enough away from the Western Front, the hospital was not overrun with wounded soldiers waiting to be treated and was able to provide a bed for Henri. Because there was nothing wrong with him, the hospital did not provide George with a bed, so he decided to sit in the hospital's reception area until he heard what, if anything, was wrong with Henri.

After a more or less sleepless night, George was approached by a doctor and asked to confirm if he had brought Henri Latour to the hospital; after he confirmed that he had, the doctor told him that Henri was suffering from the Spanish flu and would need to be kept in isolation at the hospital for the next few days to see if he would pull through. The doctor suggested to George that he come back to the hospital two or three days later, there being no question of Henri being released before then.

Much as he wanted to head for home, George could not abandon his friend and decided to stay in Paris until he knew Henri was fit enough to make his own way home. Unsure where to go or what to do, George headed to the British Embassy in Paris where he enquired about accommodation for the next few days and about getting himself home.

The walk across Paris from the hospital to the British Embassy in rue du Faubourg Saint Honore took George well over an hour; on arrival, he waited another hour before any member of the Embassy staff could see him. Once attended to, he explained that he was on his way home from a prisoner-of-war camp near Strasbourg but needed to find a bed for a couple of nights or so whilst a fellow prisoner-of-war was recovering from a fever in a Paris hospital. Because of his plight, the Embassy offered George a bed for two nights after which he would have to find somewhere else to stay; the Embassy also provided George with a small food allowance to see him through the next couple of days, it being made clear to George that, if ever he was in a position to make a contribution to the Embassy for providing him with such an allowance, he would be expected to do so.

Not expecting Henri to be released from hospital for at least forty-eight hours, George spent the time taking in the sights of Paris; with the British Embassy being located so centrally and close to the Champs Elysees, he was able to walk to Paris's main tourist attractions and, by the time he went to visit Henri two days later, he had already walked to the Arc de Triomphe on his way to the Eiffel Tower, along the left bank to Notre Dame on Ile de la Cite and across to Ile St Louis before heading back to the Embassy through the Jardin des Tuileries.

After two days of sightseeing, George returned to the hospital. On presenting himself at the hospital reception and explaining that he was there to check on Henri Latour's progress, George was asked to wait in the reception area. Some thirty minutes later George noticed a doctor heading straight towards him; the doctor stopped in front of George and asked him if he had come to enquire about Henri. On confirming that he had, George was told that the news was not good, that Henri had not recovered and had passed away the previous day, another victim of the pandemic Spanish flu virus; George was told that Henri was lying in the hospital mortuary and asked if he was willing to identify Henri. George quickly appreciated that he was probably the only person who could be contacted by the hospital officials to identify the body, so agreed to.

George had to wait another forty minutes before being escorted to the mortuary. Once George had identified Henri, it was a further thirty minutes before he had signed everything he was asked to sign. When asked what should be done with the body, George said that he was not in a position to make that decision but agreed to contact Henri's family so that a decision could be made.

Shocked by the death of his friend, George chose to head towards the Sacre Coeur Basilica at the top of Montmartre to pray and allow him time to gather his thoughts. His choice of Sacre Coeur was symbolic as its construction had only been completed the year the War started. By the time he emerged from the basilica, he had made up his mind as to what he should do. Henri's family needed to know what had come of him and how he had been a prisoner-of-war for over two years; and as George was the only person in a position to pass this information on, he knew it was his responsibility to do so. Henri's family would then be able to decide what was to happen to Henri's body.

Henri was from a village in Normandy called Barbeville, close to Bayeux. George would have to find his way there and make enquiries about Henri's family. But first he needed to return to the Embassy to collect his sparse belongings.

Embassy officials issued him with a diplomatic pass allowing him to travel free of charge on trains in France and by boat back to England.

The following morning George caught the train to Bayeux. As Barbeville was only three miles from the centre of Bayeux, George decided to walk there; an hour later, he found himself in the village square and chose the butcher's shop there to enquire where he might find the Latour family. The first response he received from one of the butchers in the shop was not too encouraging.

"Which Latour family? There must be at least three families living nearby with that name."

"I'm looking for the parents of Henri Latour. Henri would be my sort of age. I believe he lived in this village until he was called up to serve in the French Army four years ago."

The butcher spoke to one of his colleagues; George could not catch what he was saying so was unsure if the butcher was merely asking his colleague if he knew Henri or if he was seeking his confirmation that the Henri who George was referring to was the same Henri the butcher knew.

After a brief exchange with his colleague, the butcher told George that he believed the father of the Henri to whom George was referring was a widower living on the outskirts of the village, before giving directions to his house.

The house was a little over five minutes away and, although George was dreading his forthcoming meeting with Henri's family, he knew that there was no avoiding it and the longer he took to relay the sad news, the more difficult it would be for him.

George was able to locate the house he had been directed to without any difficulty; as he needed a bit of time to compose himself, it was another five minutes before George felt ready to present himself at the front door.

He knocked and waited for someone to answer. He had been expecting a man in his fifties to answer but, when the door was opened, standing in front of him was an attractive young lady who George took to be in her late teens. She asked if she could help him.

"I'm trying to locate the home of Henri Latour so I can speak to his father. Henri and I became good friends when we were in a camp together. My name is George Hart."

"Well George, you've come to the right place. I'm Isabel, Henri's sister."

"I would really like to speak to Henri's father if he's here."

"If you wait a minute, I'll get him for you. Come in and make yourself comfortable in our drawing room. Can I get you any refreshment?"

"That's kind of you. If I could trouble you for a glass of water that would be appreciated."

Isabel returned with a glass of water and, a few minutes later, a man whom George took to be Henri's father entered the drawing room; George looked to see if there was any family resemblance with Henri but, if there was any, it was not obvious.

"How can I help you?" Henri's father asked.

"Monsieur Laport, as I explained to Isabel, your son Henri and I became good friends when we were in a prisoner-of-war camp together for the last year or so. It is with much regret that I've come here to inform you that Henri passed away three days ago."

George waited for a response but none was forthcoming. Monsieur Laport was clearly thinking to himself, unclear how his son could have passed away after the War had finished. With George not knowing whether he should speak or not, Monsieur Laport eventually broke the silence.

"Monsieur Hart" the aitch being dropped in true French fashion, "are you able to explain the circumstances of his death?"

"Monsieur, when it was announced that the War was over, Henri and I decided to travel together to Paris on our ways home. During the journey, he contracted the Spanish flu. He was admitted to the St Louis hospital in Paris but sadly never recovered from the illness."

"Do you know where his body has been taken?"

"I had to identify it two days ago. He was in the hospital mortuary and I believe he's still there and will be kept there for seven days."

Monsieur Laport was lost in his thoughts, shocked at the terrible news that was passed on to him by this Englishman in front of him.

"It would be remiss of me" he said "not to thank you for going out of your way to tell me this sad, terrible news. I would like some time to myself and time with Isabel to let her know what's happened. You are no doubt keen to make your way home to your family but, before you do so, I would welcome the chance to hear more about your time with Henri. If you can delay your return home until tomorrow, you are most welcome to stay with us tonight."

Much as he was keen to be home with his family and Olivia, George knew that it would be wrong of him not to give a day of his time to Henri's family in their time of grief.

"Monsieur, that is very kind of you."

"I'll arrange for our housemaid to make up a room for you. In the meantime, if you will excuse me, I wish to speak to Isabel."

Half an hour later the housemaid arrived and beckoned George to follow her to his room. Laid out on the bed were some fresh clothes which George imagined had once been Henri's. As she left the room the housemaid informed him that Monsieur Laport would be making his way downstairs for dinner at 7:30 and would be accompanied by Isabel; George was free to use his time how he liked until then. That left a little over three hours to kill. In view of the sad news he had passed on, he made himself scarce by spending the time walking around Barbeville. There was not much to see and once George was back at the house, he kept to himself in his room until dinner.

When he felt it was time for dinner, George made his way downstairs and at the bottom of the stairs was greeted by Monsieur Laport.

"Isabel will be joining us in a few moments. Would you like a drink in the meantime?"

Seeing that Monsieur Laport already had a glass of red wine in his hand, George replied that a glass of red wine would be most welcome and, just as Monsieur Laport was pouring, Isabel joined them in the drawing room. She had changed for dinner and, whereas George had been taken by her attractiveness when he had first met her earlier that day, he now saw before him a young lady whose beauty stood out.

Over dinner, he recounted his time with Henri in the prisoner-of-war camp and how they had helped each other with the other's language and become good friends. He was able to pass on what Henri had told him about his capture in October 1916 during the battle of Verdun.

"Isabel and I are most grateful that you have gone so much out of your way to tell us about Henri" said Monsieur Laport as he helped himself to a piece of local camembert being offered by the housemaid. We'll never be able to thank you enough, even though the news you have passed on to us is so unwelcome. We could not be sure if Henri would survive the War but to have survived the War and then be struck down by illness within days of it ending is not easy to accept. What a terrible irony. We of course had hoped and prayed that Henri would survive but our hopes and prayers seem to have been answered then cruelly dashed. I had hoped that Henri would return safely in one piece and that we could work and build up a business together but that cannot now happen."

"Papa, maybe I could be your business partner" said Isabel.

"Isabel, that would be wonderful but what will happen when you get married and have children?"

"Who says I'll get married and have children?"

"I do because you are too beautiful and too good a person not to be married."

"But Papa, I need to find the right man to marry and with so many men lost in the War, how can you be sure I'll find one? I don't think I'm likely to find one if I stay at home."

George was keen to change the subject as he thought this was a family matter but all he could think of asking was what line of business Monsieur Laport was in.

"Before the outbreak of war, my wife and I ran a small hotel business; we owned a hotel in Bayeux but once war broke out, we closed it down. Sadly my wife died nearly two years ago but now the War is over, I'll think about opening it up again. If I make a success of it, I'd consider expanding the business by acquiring other hotels in Normandy and perhaps Brittany. I think there'll be demand for hotel accommodation in attractive seaside towns but before I think too far ahead, I need to make sure I make a success of our hotel in Bayeux. I don't know what Henri was planning for his future but it would have been easy for me to include him in the business."

This response prompted Isabel to interject "Instead you'll have me, someone who, like Maman, will be able to add a more feminine touch to the business."

"Indeed, Isabel. You could prove to be a great asset to the business; that is until you go off and get yourself married."

Monsieur Laport chose this moment to ask George about his plans.

"Monsieur, I've not given much thought to what I'll do. When I enrolled in the Royal Flying Corps, I still had over a year of my university course to complete but I don't know if my place will still be open and, even if it is, I don't know if I'll have the appetite or will to complete it. I can't believe life back in England will be the same as it was and I guess I'll just have to acclimatise myself to civilian life again when I'm back home before making any decisions. I've no idea what jobs will be available for someone like me, and even if jobs are available, whether I have the right experience for such jobs and whether they'll suit me."

"George, I have no doubt life will be different but I'm sure that to have survived what you've been through for the last couple of years will put you in good stead for your future, wherever it may take you. Without necessarily recognising it yourself, you'll have matured in a way which would have been very different had you spent the last couple of years still at university. And what about your immediate plans?"

"I need to make my way home. I had planned to get a train from Paris but, now that I'm here, I suppose I might just as well make my way to Cherbourg or Le Havre and see if I can catch a ferry to the south coast of England. What would you recommend?"

"I can make enquiries in the morning to see what ferry services are operating. It may well be that the quickest way back to England from here will be to return via Paris but, if it can wait, I'll find out what I can in the morning. Of course, if you do have to return via Paris, I will accompany you to Paris as I have to make appropriate arrangements for Henri."

"If you could make enquiries on my behalf, that would be most kind of you; I wouldn't want to make my way to a port only to find there are no boats going in the right direction."

After they had finished dinner, Monsieur Laport asked George and Isabel if they minded excusing him, the emotions of the day catching up with him. George expected Isabel to ask if she too could be excused but, instead, she asked him if he would like to join her in the drawing room for a nightcap. Tired as he was, George thought it would be rude to decline her offer.

"Yes, it would be my pleasure."

"What would you like to drink?"

"What are you offering?"

"My father usually has some cognac available but maybe I can tempt you with a glass of Calvados."

"What's that?"

"Calvados is a type of brandy with an apple flavour; in Brittany and Normandy it is a popular liqueur because it's from this area."

"In which case, I'd like to try a glass."

Isabel poured George a glass and one for herself. He took a small sip to start with but once he realised it was not going to poison him, was able to relax more and enjoy the drink. It did not take him much time to empty his glass and, when he had done so, Isabel asked him if he would like another one. He replied saying he would like one more but promised it would be his last one for the night.

Not wanting to cause Isabel any more sorrow, George kept Henri out of his conversation with her but instead asked her about her plans and whether she meant it when she said she could work with her father. Isabel told him that, before the War, her father and mother had worked together and she could see no reason why she could not do the same. In Isabel's view, following the death of her mother, she was the ideal person to help out her father whose strength was more as a strategist than as a doer. Isabel also confessed that she did not want another woman in her father's life and one way to minimise that risk would be for her to work with him rather than for some other woman to.

Enjoying her company, George took more time over his second glass of Calvados but when Isabel noticed he had finished it, she told him it was time for her to retire to bed. George said that it was time for him to retire as well; it had been a long day for him and, although he had witnessed many deaths during the War, today was the first time he had passed on the news of a death to a deceased's relatives, an experience he hoped he would never have to repeat.

Once in his room, he had no difficulty falling asleep as the bed he was sleeping in was by far the most comfortable he had slept in for quite some time but he had a troubled night with a couple of disturbing dreams. One had been about getting home to his parents only for them to be away; perhaps it was on his conscience that he should have made more of an effort to have made it home by now. The other dream concerned Isabel and Olivia, arguing with each other, each of them claiming that George was hers; George had spent much of his time in captivity thinking about Olivia but as the War dragged on the memories became more distant and, since the War had ended, he had been too pre-occupied with Henri to think about when he would see her again.

In the morning Isabel asked him how he had slept; rather than tell her truth, he told her that he had slept well. He knew not to tell her about the dream he had had about her, not least because it would have been so presumptuous for him to assume after having known her for only one day that she might be possessive about him.

Later that morning Monsieur Laport told him that his prospects of picking up a boat from a nearby port heading for England were not good and that he would be better off heading back to Paris and picking up a train to take him to Boulogne or Calais where he was much more likely to find a passage across the Channel. Monsieur Laport also told George that he had made arrangements to travel to Paris the next day to sort things out about Henri and he would welcome George's company for the journey; much as George was keen to get back home as soon as possible, he felt he could not decline this offer.

Not sure how he was going to pass the time before travelling to Paris the next day, George readily accepted Isabel's invitation that he accompany her on her trip that day to Bayeux to buy provisions for the house, a responsibility Isabel had assumed following the death of her mother. As George knew from when he made the journey to the Latour home the previous day, it would take them two hours there and back and George was keen to spend his time with the Latours with something to do.

They were away for the best part of the day; after Isabel had finished buying everything she felt was needed for the home, she asked George if he would like some refreshment before heading home, an offer George was only too keen to accept after traipsing around more shops than he cared for. Isabel too looked as if she could do with the rest. She took him to a café and ordered a glass of kir for each of them. Although it was not the refreshing drink George had in mind, he was not inclined to object even though he had no idea what kir was and only ever rarely drank alcohol during the day. Despite this, he enjoyed the kir and one glass was enough to make him relax more in Isabel's company.

Over their glasses of kir and on the walk back, Isabel talked about Henri and how close they had been during their childhood. George found himself doing more of the listening than the talking but when the opportunity arose, he told Isabel that, during their time in camp together, Henri had spoken to him in much the same way about Isabel as she did about Henri. George was in no doubt that Isabel would need time to come to terms with the death of Henri and he was more than willing to be her sounding board if she wanted to talk about her brother.

That evening was spent in much the same way as the previous evening with a formal dinner being served, at the end of which Isabel's father retired leaving the two of them alone. After her father retired, Isabel asked George if he could face a glass of Calvados again but George declined, opting for a cognac instead. This time together, it was Isabel's turn to ask about George's life before the War; George talked openly to Isabel about his parents, his brother and his time at school but when he spoke about his time at university, he made no mention of Olivia. It was only later when he had retired to bed that he questioned himself why he had not spoken about her; was it because he thought it inappropriate to do so or was it because he did not want Isabel to think there was someone else in his life? It had taken no time for George to realise he enjoyed Isabel's company and he did not want to jeopardise their friendship but he was not sure whether, by not speaking about Olivia, he was protecting himself or he was protecting Isabel.

In the morning, George and Monsieur Laport made their way to Bayeux to catch the Paris train. Before his departure, Isabel bade George farewell wishing him a safe journey. Just as he was ready to depart, Isabel kissed him on the cheek and told him that she hoped their paths would cross again; George too hoped for the same but doubted that they ever would.

The train journey to Paris was slow but the time seemed to pass more quickly than the outward journey as George had company with whom he conversed for much of the journey. He questioned

Monsieur Laport about his business and his plans for it and put in a good word for Isabel, confident that she had more to offer her father in running his business than he had intimated. In response, Monsieur Laport confided that he had little doubt that Isabel could be of great assistance but his main concern was that, once she was married and had children, she would be drawn away from the business and replacing her would not be easy.

Disembarking at Gare St Lazare, they knew this was when they would be going their separate ways.

"George, I'm indebted to you and can't thank you enough for the trouble you've taken to tell me not only the tragic news of Henri's death but also what happened to him in the War and how he survived it. I only wish that there was a way I could show my gratitude."

"Monsieur Laport, I too have lost a good friend and I owed it to him to let his family know what became of him."

"I ask only one more favour of you. If ever you are visiting France in the future, please ensure you come and see us again. It would mean a lot to me and I suspect it would mean a lot more to Isabel than she would ever let on. In the short time we've both known you, we can understand why you and Henri became good friends and keeping in touch will allow us, during times of sadness, to reflect on happier times. I wish you a bon voyage."

"Thank you Monsieur. I promise you that I shall come and see you again."

George then made his way to Gare du Nord to catch the first train heading for Boulogne or Calais. At the station, there were a number of British servicemen making their way back to England; some had only just arrived in Paris whilst others had chosen to spend their first few days away from the fighting enjoying some of the spoils on offer in the city.

George had to wait a little over an hour before boarding a train bound for Calais. Once aboard, other passengers assured him that, once in Calais, there would be plenty of boats waiting to transport them across the Channel. On its way to Calais the train stopped at Boulogne but he resisted the temptation to disembark there, trusting the advice of his fellow passengers that Calais would be a better bet for picking up a ride to take him across the Channel. Once in Calais, he made his way to the docks to discover that he was just one of many making their way home from the War. Darkness had already fallen and, after a long day travelling, he was happy to leave it until the next day to see if there would be any boats he could board for the journey to Dover.

After spending the night in a hostel near the docks, George headed back to the docks at first light the following morning; arrangements for transporting servicemen back home seemed more organised than the previous evening and George found himself designated to a boat due to leave Calais bound for Dover at one o'clock that afternoon. It was not until just after midday that he was able to board the boat and, although it had been scheduled to leave at one, it was another hour before the boat started up its engines to make the crossing.

Although it was winter time, the crossing was relatively calm, allowing the boat to make the twenty-one mile journey in a little under three hours. On arrival on Dover, George was desperate to telephone his parents to tell them he had arrived home safely and would be with them shortly but, with no telephone kiosks in sight, he decided to wait until he arrived in London to see if he could find one there.

By the time he had arrived at Victoria Station, it was after 8 o'clock in the evening but he was determined to make it home to his parents that night. On his way to Waterloo to catch a train heading in the direction of Barnes, George went into the first hotel he passed and asked if he could borrow the hotel's telephone to make a call to his parents; the hotel manager was reluctant to agree to this until George explained that he was returning home from the War having spent the best part of a year as a prisoner-of-war and wanted to assure his parents he was still alive.

George dialled his parents' number. On the sixth ring, his father picked up the phone and asked who was calling.

"Father, it's your son."

"Is that you Edward? What are calling for at this time of night? Is everything alright?"

"No father, it's George speaking. I'm on my way to Waterloo to catch a train back home."

George's father could not believe what he was hearing. "Is that really you George?"

"Yes father and I should be with you shortly."

"George, don't get the train. Get a taxi and we'll pay for it when it arrives. I'm sorry if I sound a bit mystified but we'll explain when you get home. This is such wonderful news. Your mother and I cannot wait to see you."

"Well father, you'll just have to be patient. I'll be with you as quickly as I can. I can't wait to see the two of you either."

Much as George's parents were overwhelmed with the news that George was alive and had returned home safely, they were in no doubt that his return would cause complications. They knew that they would have to tell George about Edward's marriage to Olivia but questioned whether they needed to tell him about Jill, the daughter he would not have known he had. Over the first few days of his return, George talked about his capture and time as a prisoner-of-war but he was just as keen to hear how his parents had fared and news about Edward.

George's parents waited a couple of days before breaking the news about Edward marrying Olivia. They did their best to play it down, suggesting that it was more a marriage of convenience than one of love, with each of them seeking comfort in the mistaken belief that George was dead. Devastated by such news, George questioned his parents how Edward and Olivia could do such a thing and how his parents could allow Edward to do such a thing. Their answers brought no comfort to George who felt betrayed by his own family.

George's reaction did not come as a surprise to his parents but it was such that they knew that now was not the time to break the news to him about his daughter Jill.

The shocking news also caused George not to want to see his brother for fear of what he might say to him. With Christmas only a month away, he was not sure he could avoid seeing him as Edward would be visiting his parents at some time over the Christmas period even if he would not be spending Christmas with them. George realised that he would have to make a decision about his future within the next few weeks if, as seemed likely, that future involved keeping apart from his one and only brother.

Much as he was shaken and upset about his brother marrying the love of his life, George accepted that there was nothing he could do to change it. Even if his wartime experiences made him appreciate there were far worse things in life, it was also not something he wanted to be reminded constantly about and his thoughts turned to what he might do. He considered returning to university to finish his degree but discounted it because he saw little value in doing so; he also wondered how he would cope with memories of his time there with Olivia. Another option was to find work in the City of London but he felt that eventually his and Edward's paths would cross, something he was not yet ready for.

With time on his hands, his mind started wandering. His thoughts turned to France and the Laport family. Maybe he would be able to provide Monsieur Laport with the support in running his business that he had been expecting of Henri. What did he have to lose by exploring this opportunity, even if it was only a long shot? If nothing came of it, he would be no worse off than if he stayed at home. Feeling unwanted at home, he headed back to France to offer his services to Monsieur Laport. Although George's parents tried to talk him out it, their efforts were never more than half-hearted as, much as they did not want to lose George again, they recognised that it provided a solution to a difficult family situation.

Less than two weeks after having returned home, George found himself heading back to France, the only dilemma facing George's parents as he left being whether or not to tell Edward that his brother had survived the War.

Part 5

December 1918-1923

Isabel was just finishing her lunch when she heard a knock on the front door. As she was the only person in the house at the time, she answered the door and much to her surprise standing there in front of her was George.

"What are you doing here?" she enquired. In trying to disguise her pleasure in seeing him, her voice came across differently to how she would have liked, hoping it had not sounded unwelcoming.

"Well, when I got home, everything seemed different. I couldn't think what to do with myself, so I wondered if I could be of assistance to your father in his business" George replied, without explaining what had seemed so different back home. He had decided not to write to warn Isabel and her father that he was planning to visit them as it would have taken time before he heard back from them and he believed it would be more difficult for Isabel's father to refuse his proposition face to face than by letter.

"I can't speak for my father so you'll have to speak to him about that."

She was pleased to see him again and to lighten things up, added "Just so long as you don't persuade him to take you on at my expense. He's not at home at the moment but should be back later this afternoon. In the meantime do please come inside and join me whilst I finish my lunch."

As George had not eaten since breakfast that morning, he accepted Isabel's invitation as well as her offer to provide him with lunch. Over lunch and before Isabel's father returned, George asked her about her father's visit to Paris to deal with Henri and his effects; she told him that her father had not found it easy and, to avoid the complications of returning the body to be buried near home, had arranged for a simple burial at the Pere Lachaise cemetery, not far from the hospital where Henri had died.

When he returned later that afternoon, Monsieur Laport was surprised to see George and, like Isabel, interested to hear why he was there. As had been the case with Isabel, George chose not to explain the reason he no longer wanted to stay in England was because his brother had married the girl he had loved before he went off to war, albeit in the belief George was dead. Instead, he explained to Monsieur Laport that once he was back home he realised he had no idea what he wanted to do but, with Henri no longer around to help, perhaps his family's hotel business could do with a spare pair of hands.

Since the War had come to an end, Monsieur Laport had not given much thought to how he was planning to run his hotel, having come to the view that the business was unlikely to attract enough customers to make it viable before the following spring. Having relayed this information to George, he also told him that he would like a few days to think about it but, in the meantime, George was most welcome and should make himself feel at home.

George took the opportunity during the time he was waiting for an answer to see what the prospects were for other jobs in the region and discovered that, due to the loss of life in the War, many of the local businesses were looking for an extra pair of hands to carry out any number of jobs, ranging from delivery men to builders to office clerks. George was confident that, if he wanted to find work, there was enough around. George also spent a fair amount of the time waiting for Monsieur Laport's answer in the company of Isabel and the more time they spent together the more he enjoyed her company; and the more he enjoyed her company the more he found himself attracted to her. However, he kept that to himself as he had no idea how she felt about him and the right time to reveal any interest in her other than a platonic one was not whilst she was grieving the loss of her brother; he also needed time to come to terms with what he still felt was a betrayal on the part of his family and Olivia.

It took Monsieur Laport four days before he gave George his answer.

"George, I've given much thought to your kind offer and I apologise for taking the time that it has to let you know my answer. In some ways, I'm grateful to you for your proposal because it's required me to think about building up the business again. Because of this and because I'll need an extra pair of hands, I'm willing to offer you a position working with me. However, I don't anticipate the hotel re-opening or generating any revenue before spring next year. In view of this, I'm not going to be able to offer you anything in the way of a salary but I can offer you board and lodging here. I appreciate that you may want to earn some money for yourself, so I'd encourage you to look for other work which will pay you."

The lack of pay being offered by Monsieur Laport did not unduly worry George as he had no other plans.

"Monsieur Laport, I'm most grateful for your kind offer which I have no hesitation in accepting. I appreciate your suggestion that I seek paid work as well but I shall only do so if you're unable to find enough work for me to keep me fully occupied."

"That is excellent news. With Christmas only days away, may I suggest that we wait until the New Year before we give more serious thought to planning the hotel's future. Nothing will happen between now and then and it'll give us time to get to know each other better".

Monsieur Laport, Isabel and George spent Christmas together. Although Isabel cooked a delicious meal washed down with some excellent wines which Monsieur Laport produced, none of the three of them felt the occasion was one for celebration with the loss of Henri casting a shadow over the day. Because of that, Monsieur Laport insisted that they make more of New Year's Eve and, as the start of 1919 approached, having consumed more wine than he was used to drinking, he raised a glass first to toast Henri and then to post-war prosperity with his new business colleague George.

The following day Monsieur Laport took George to his hotel in Bayeux. It had been closed for two years and, although Monsieur Laport had visited it frequently in the meantime, he knew much was needed to get it up and running again. On arrival at the hotel, George could see from the exterior that it would have been one of Bayeux's smarter hotels, if not its smartest, which was confirmed following his tour of the interior. Although there were only twenty bedrooms, they were all spacious as was the dining room and bar area. George could see the hotel had the potential to return to its former glory but would require a lot of hard work and a bit of money. After the tour, Monsieur Laport asked George for his views.

"Well, Monsieur, my initial impression is that, although the property is not currently looking its best for understandable reasons, it could be restored to become somewhere where the guests feel very comfortable. So, as far as the property is concerned, I think it's ideal. However, its success will depend upon whether it can attract guests who will want to come to Bayeux and stay in such comfort and that in turn will depend in part upon what else Bayeux has to offer, both in terms of other hotel accommodation and tourist attractions. In my opinion, the key issue will be to ensure that the money that is spent on improving the current condition of the hotel is spent in such a way which will attract enough guests to justify the cost".

George had not meant to sound pessimistic but he had no idea what the likely demand for an up-market hotel in Bayeux would be now the War was over.

"George, thank you for sharing with me your honest view. You are of course understandably cautious and I admire that.

I can assure you though that, before the War, the hotel was run profitably and, even though I understand the War may cause many to consider how they spend their money and what to spend it on, there are still plenty of wealthy people in France who will want to spend their time and money in much the same way as they did before the War. I'm therefore confident that a premier hotel in Bayeux will be able to attract the sort of clientele that the hotel should be targeting and that clientele will be, to a large extent, the same as it was before the War".

"What clientele was that?"

"Mostly wealthy Parisians."

"What makes you confident that they'll continue to want to come and stay in Bayeux?"

"For many of them, the War prevented them enjoying the opulent lifestyle they were used to before the War. I believe the best way they'll be able to forget the miseries they encountered during the war years will be to return to the way of life they indulged themselves in before the War."

Although George did not share Monsieur Laport's confidence neither did he feel able to challenge it. Instead, he was happy to go along with it as he had nothing to lose by doing so and was keen to get started assisting as best he could in seeing the hotel return to being the most sought-after hotel for guests visiting the area.

Over the next couple of months, George undertook a variety of tasks all of which were new to him but it did not take him long to get the hang of stripping wallpaper, wallpapering, painting walls and sandpapering and by early March, the hotel was showing a marked improvement. He had also been given responsibility for tidying up the hotel's grounds, whilst Isabel was applying the finishing touches to the hotel's interior.

Although the hotel was ready for opening by the end of March, Monsieur Laport was keen for there to be a grand opening and chose Saturday 31st May for the occasion. This gave them two months to plan the event. In order to show the renovated hotel to as many potential customers as possible, the three of them agreed that the formal opening should not be a sit-down dinner as the dining room would not be able to accommodate everyone they wanted to invite but instead would be a champagne reception with canapes and dancing to follow. The guest list was divided into two, with one list consisting of VIPs in the Bayeux area and the other list consisting of former hotel guests most of whom were from further afield. As George had not been in contact with his parents since leaving them in December, he asked if they could be included on the guest list, something both Monsieur Laport and Isabel agreed would be a wonderful idea; they were keen to attract overseas guests and in particular those from across the Channel and it had crossed their minds that George's family might be a useful source for introducing English guests.

When sending the invitation to his parents, George wrote telling them what he had been up to since December; he also took the opportunity to tell them that, even with the passing of time, he had still not fully come to terms with what had happened with Edward and Olivia and that, as a consequence, he was, at least for the time being, happy to try his hand in the hotel business in France. In their reply his parents thanked him for his letter and the invitation but told him that regretfully they were unable to accept it but added that they hoped there would be an opportunity to visit him in France later in the year, perhaps during the summer. On receiving their reply, George felt relieved as if some barrier between him and his parents had been removed, prompting him to ensure that he wrote to them on a more frequent basis.

Rooms for the opening reception were available on a "first come first served" basis, with three rooms being reserved for Monsieur Laport, Isabel and George. The other seventeen rooms were booked up by guests well ahead of the reception and of the one hundred and fifty guests invited, there were just over one hundred acceptances, with most of those declining being invitees from further afield than Normandy. As only champagne with canapes and dancing were planned, organising the reception was relatively straightforward but Monsieur Laport was keen to ensure the evening passed faultlessly and for this to happen, he insisted that there was enough staff on hand to ensure all of the guests had enough to eat and none of them had an empty glass. He trusted his chefs to come up with enough canapes and chose his favourite champagne, Taittinger, for the occasion.

The guests were invited to arrive from 7 o'clock in the evening and, by 8 o'clock, all those expected had arrived. Although George had been working and living near Bayeux for the best part of six months, he had only met a small number of the guests whereas all of them were known to Monsieur Laport and most of them to Isabel. As a consequence, it was easier for Monsieur Laport and Isabel to mingle with the guests as George watched on. The band was due to start playing at 9 o'clock but before it was permitted to do so, Monsieur Laport said a few words to welcome his guests.

"Mesdames et Messieurs, welcome to the official re-opening of the Laport Hotel. It was with much regret that the War forced us to close temporarily but we are now open again for business and I look forward to welcoming you as guests. Before I ask the band to commence playing and the dancing to begin, please raise your glasses as I toast the many whose lives were lost in the War, to peace in France and to the Republic. To the many, to peace and to the Republic."

As the guests joined in the toast, Monsieur Laport signalled to the band to start. For many of the guests, the evening was their first evening out in a number of years and, with plenty of champagne inside them, they took to the dance floor as if it were the last time they would ever dance. The band played a variety of music allowing the guests to show off their ballroom skills to dances such as the polka, the foxtrot and the tango. It was clearly Monsieur Laport's ambition to try and dance with as many of his female guests as he could and whilst George played more the part of a wallflower, Isabel never seemed short of a partner.

Just before the music was coming to an end for the evening, Isabel approached George and asked him whether he was going to ask her for a dance. He knew there was no way he could say no, not that he wanted to and replied telling her that he would be delighted if he could have the pleasure of the next dance with her. As they arrived on the dance floor, the band started playing music to foxtrot to and George was grateful that he could remember the basis steps from years back when his mother had made him take ballroom dance classes. As the dance ended, the band announced that the next dance would be the final one for the evening and, as they started playing music to waltz to, Isabel intimated to George that she would like to share this dance with him as well. Despite having lived together in the same house for nearly six months, Isabel had not shown any signs that she was interested in George other than platonically as a colleague but by the time the waltz came to an end, George had reason to think otherwise.

Not long after the music stopped, those guests not staying at the hotel made their way home whilst those staying made their way to their rooms. Monsieur Laport, Isabel and George stayed up until all the guests and the band players had departed; feeling he could relax for the first time that evening, Monsieur Laport insisted Isabel and George join him for a final glass of champagne before retiring for the night. He thanked both of them for being such an attentive host and hostess and was keen to hear their views on how they thought the evening had gone. Isabel told her father she thought the evening had been a success, with those present seeming to enjoy themselves and to enjoy the opportunity to party again; George added that he too thought the evening was a success.

After they had finished their glasses of champagne, they made their way upstairs to their rooms for the night. On reaching Monsieur Laport's room, Isabel kissed him on both cheeks and wished him a good night's sleep. George then escorted Isabel to her room and as she entered her room, turned and gave him a light kiss brushing his lips. George was not sure how to react to what was clearly a more intimate kiss than she had given her father; nor did he know how she would react if he responded with an even more intimate kiss, so thought better of it – if his relationship with Isabel was to develop into a more physical one, there would be plenty of time for that.

Monsieur Laport spent much of the following day talking to those guests who had stayed overnight, eager to persuade them to make bookings during the summer. Most were unwilling to commit there and then but nearly all promised they would come and stay again before too long.

Over the course of the summer months, many of the guests kept to their word and spent a week at the hotel. Monsieur Laport knew though that the future success and viability of the hotel could not be judged on the first summer after it had re-opened, recognising that it would take time for the hotel's reputation to spread. Throughout the period, Monsieur Laport, Isabel and George worked endlessly at ensuring the guests had every comfort, not just to encourage repeat business but out of pride as well.

Two guests who came to stay over a weekend towards the end of September were George's parents who had travelled to Bayeux by train via Paris. With the hotel not being full, Monsieur Laport allowed George to stay at the hotel and take the weekend off so that he could spend the time with them. During their visit, George showed them the more interesting of the local sights which included a trip to the seaside at Arromanches-les-Bains, less than ten miles away. Over dinner, as they each caught up with each other's news, George thought it was only right that he should ask after Edward and Olivia, in reply to which George's father said little other than to say they were keeping well.

"Do they know I survived the War?"

George's father answered. "We thought long and hard about telling them and in the end we thought it only right that we should tell Edward. We also thought it right that we should leave it to him to decide about whether or not Olivia should know."

"D'you know if he told Olivia?"

"We don't know but we think not, as we like to believe she'd have mentioned it to us if she knew."

During their visit, George introduced his parents to Monsieur Laport and Isabel, who insisted that George and his parents join them at their home for dinner one evening. Over the course of their meal, Monsieur Laport asked Mr and Mrs Hart about their family, including about Edward. Monsieur Laport and Isabel knew that George had a brother whom he never spoke about but Monsieur Laport thought it would be impolite not to ask about him. When asked whether Edward had a family of his own, George's father could see the discomfort such a question caused George and replied that he did not and because of his war wounds was not expected to, choosing to make no mention of Jill, George's daughter and Edward's step-daughter.

George's parents were due to make their way home to England the following day and, before doing so, asked George if he planned to make a trip home himself, hoping he would do so before too long. George told them that, even though he would like to, he knew it could cause complications if he were to see Edward and Olivia and he felt that he was not quite ready for this. He asked for more time to come to terms with what had happened, giving them hope that there might be some form of reconciliation at some stage in the future.

As George bade his parents farewell, they were all saddened by the parting knowing it would be many months before they were likely to see each other again. George promised to write home every month and told his parents that he looked forward to hearing from them as well.

That afternoon, recognising George was sorry to see his parents leave, Isabel sought him out to try and comfort him.

"I'm so glad to have met your parents; they're a charming couple."

"Thank you. It was good to see them and I know they appreciated your hospitality."

"You should try and see them more often. Why don't you take some time off and visit them in England? Perhaps you could take me? I've never been to England."

George looked Isabel in the eye to see if she was being serious or just flirtatious; he could not tell which or whether it was both.

"Do you mean that?"

"Of course I do. When would be a good time?"

"Any time really but I think England looks her best in May."

"Right then; tell your parents you're planning to come to England next May and that you'll be taking me with you. That's settled then."

Later that day, after their evening meal and after Monsieur Laport had retired for the evening, Isabel asked George why he never talked about his brother.

"It's complicated."

"Why's it complicated? If it's complicated, might you not feel better about it if you shared it with someone?"

George paused. "Something happened between us which made me feel very let down."

"It must've been serious for you to keep it bottled up in the way you have for so many months."

"It was very serious but I don't think I should burden you with it."

"Why not? We're good friends, aren't we? And why can't you share it with a good friend?"

"Alright, I'll tell you. Pour me a glass of brandy first."

She disappeared to find him a glass of brandy and George drew a deep breath as he contemplated how much he should tell her. When she returned and handed him his brandy, she sat opposite him as he took a large sip.

"Whilst we were growing up," he started "my brother and I were very close; I think he looked up to me as I was older than him. Unfortunately, the War changed everything. Before I signed up, I had been courting a young lady and we had talked about getting married once the War was over. When my plane was shot down, none of my colleagues witnessed it and it was therefore presumed that I was dead and this was what was reported to my parents. My brother also survived the War but sustained injuries and was sent back to England to convalesce. In the hospital in which my brother was convalescing, one of the nurses recognised him. In the belief that I was dead, they grieved together and found comfort with each other. When I arrived back in England after the War, I was told that they'd married. The nurse in question was the girl I had thought I would marry one day. Instead, it transpired that she'd married my younger brother. So, knowing the embarrassment it could cause if I stayed at home, I had to find somewhere else to live and decided to try my luck here."

As Isabel took in what George had just told her, she stood up and wandered over to the chair George was sitting in and, after sitting herself on his lap, put her arms around him and drew him towards her. She knew there was nothing she could say to console him but she hoped that an affectionate hug would provide George with some form of comfort she was not able to put into words. Neither of them moved until George turned to look into her eyes, choosing this moment to kiss her firmly on her lips, something to which Isabel was most receptive. They stayed there together for several minutes before either of them spoke. Finally Isabel broke the silence between them.

"After all you went through in the War, it must have been so hard for you to take."

"It was at first but recognising how much families suffered because of the War, including your own, made it easier for me to come to terms with it. Although I felt betrayed, I knew I had so much more to look forward to than a good many other people."

"Thank you for telling me. I hope it'll help having spoken about it to someone and you don't think it was out of place for me to ask you."

"No, I don't. Perhaps I needed to get it off my chest and put it behind me more than I've managed to date. And I hope you don't mind me kissing you."

"No, not at all, unless it meant nothing to you."

"I can assure you it meant plenty to me. So too has the time I have spent with you and your father – both of you have helped me move on and I am indebted to both of you for it."

"You don't owe us anything. If anything, we owe you for the care you took of Henri, providing him with comradeship in prison and helping him when he was ill."

"Enough of that. Let's say honours are even. And on that note, I think now would be an appropriate time for us both to retire for the night."

Isabel gave George one last hug before she stood up and then one last kiss on the cheek before heading off to bed. "Sleep well and think of me."

"I shall. I hope you sleep well too."

As the summer season came to an end, business at the hotel slowed down and, rather than try and fill the rooms during the off-season period, Monsieur Laport concentrated more on the hotel's restaurant to attract business. He knew that it was unrealistic to expect the restaurant to be busy every lunchtime and every evening so he staggered the opening times with lunch served only on Wednesdays and Sundays and dinner served only on Fridays and Saturdays; key to the restaurant's success was the quality of food and the quality of service and it was not long before the restaurant earned the reputation of being the best place to eat for miles around.

Although the restaurant stayed open during the winter months, Monsieur Laport decided not to take hotel bookings for the period from the end of October until April the following year and instead used the winter months to promote the hotel business for when it re-opened. Information about the hotel was sent to all those who had stayed there prior to its closure and slowly but surely advance bookings were taken for 1920. George's relationship with Isabel was also developing but they were both mindful that any public shows of affection at the hotel would come across as unprofessional and they kept their feelings for each other private, even to the extent that Monsieur Laport was unaware that their feelings for each other were growing.

When George and Isabel broached the subject of the two of them paying a visit to London in May, Monsieur Laport wondered whether their relationship was more than just a platonic one but kept his thoughts to himself. Instead, he pointed out to them that, if they were planning such a trip, it might be better to make it in March before the hotel re-opened in the spring but subject to this, he was all in favour of them having some time to themselves before what he hoped would be a busy few months for them both.

They opted to travel via Paris with a ferry crossing from Calais rather than risk a longer crossing from Cherbourg in potentially rougher conditions. When hearing of their plan, Monsieur Laport was keen that they spent some time in Paris to promote the hotel, although at first George and Isabel were not sure what he had in mind nor how they should go about this.

By the time they set off in mid-March, they had decided upon their strategy for promoting the hotel; one part involved inviting to a cocktail party at the hotel George and Isabel were staying in all those Parisians who had been invited to Monsieur Laport's hotel re-opening reception held in May the previous year who had been unable to attend, and the other part involved arranging meetings with journalists who worked for the newspapers whose readership they thought would be most attracted to the hotel.

The reception, which included a brief introduction from Isabel, was well received by those who attended and enough interest was shown for George and Isabel to feel confident that some of the guests would visit Monsieur Laport's hotel in the summer. With the journalists, they targeted a number of newspapers ranging from the rather serious *Le Temps* to the more moderate *Le Figaro* and to the more gossipy *Le Petit Journal* and *Le Petit Parisien*. George felt that all the journalists only took interest in listening to what Isabel had to say but he was not one to question why she appealed to them more than he did if it was going to generate publicity and business for the hotel. It was also clear to George that reports about the hotel by the journalists were more likely to be favourable if they stayed there so offers of free nights were made to each of the four journalists they met.

Although not particularly rough, the ferry crossing to Dover was rough enough for them to appreciate that their choice of a Channel crossing from Calais rather than the longer one from Cherbourg was a wise one. At Dover, they took the train to London Victoria and then the tube to Hammersmith where they boarded a bus to Barnes. On the journey, Isabel enquired whether she would meet Edward during their trip but George thought this unlikely.

During their three-day visit, they spent the days visiting London's best known tourist attractions, including the Tower of London, Tower Bridge close by, St Paul's Cathedral, the Houses of Parliament and Trafalgar Square. One evening, they went to a show in the West End but otherwise the evenings were spent with George's parents at home. George's parents had not included Edward in any of their plans for George and Isabel so Isabel did not get to meet him, Isabel's only regret as the visit came to an end. Because it was the first time the two of them had had time together away from the hotel and away from Isabel's father, they had been able to relax in each other's company more than normal.

The return trip to Bayeux could not be done in one day so they broke the journey in Paris. Much as Isabel had enjoyed her first visit to London, she felt it lacked the intimacy of Paris; with London so much more spread out, she felt it also missed some of the romanticism that Paris offered. In Paris, they looked for a hotel close to the river but not too far from Gare St-Lazare, the station from which they would be catching the train back to Bayeux the following morning. Eventually they settled on a hotel off the Boulevard Malesherbes and just as George was about to enquire of the receptionist if the hotel had two single rooms, Isabel butted in and asked if there was a vacancy for a double room for the night. George was too stunned to question or contradict her request. George knew that he would have to keep his thoughts to himself as they were escorted to their double room by the hotel porter but once they were alone in the room, he turned to Isabel.

"Are you mad? What on earth will your father think if he ever finds out we shared a room together?"

"George, I don't intend to tell him and I'm assuming you're not planning to either."

"No, of course I'm not but what will he do if he finds out?"

"I don't think you need be too worried about that; it is down to us to make sure he never does. If on the other hand you would prefer to be in a separate room, I can speak to the receptionist."

"No, it's not that; it's just that we've never spoken about spending a night together and it's taken me somewhat by surprise."

"George, I don't know if it's just your Englishness but can you not tell that I've fallen in love with you? Have you not noticed that I don't see or spend any of my time with other men? The reason for that is quite simply the only man I'm interested in is you."

"Isabel, I'm very fond of you and I enjoy being with you. Perhaps what you put down to my Englishness is more a case of the respect I have for your father, who employs us."

"That hasn't stopped us having the occasional passionate kiss so why should your respect for my father stop our relationship from going beyond just passionate kisses and becoming more intimate?"

George paused before answering.

"You're right; there's no reason why it should."

"It's not because you still have feelings for Olivia, is it?"

"Good heavens, not at all. It is, as I say, because of the respect I have for your father and my concern that he'll think I'm taking advantage of his very special daughter."

As reassured as she was by his answer about Olivia, Isabel felt that there was still work to be done to win over George's heart. She decided the best way to do this would be to ensure she did not make herself too easily available by throwing herself at him but instead play hard to get, but with enough encouragement to make him realise it would be worth the effort. As if to make her point, she gave him a quick kiss on the cheek before suggesting that they both needed something to eat and that it was therefore time to venture out and find a suitable restaurant nearby.

Over dinner at a brasserie recommended by the hotel receptionist, George was quieter than normal; although Isabel had told him that she had fallen in love with him and although he found this flattering, he was not sure what he had done to earn her affection; nor did he feel that his fondness for Isabel constituted love or, if it did, it was very different to what he had felt when he had been in love with Olivia. Even though he had denied continuing to have any feelings for Olivia, being reminded of her did make him wonder whether he did still have feelings for her. Noticing his apparent reluctance to converse, Isabel asked him if he was feeling alright.

"Why d'you ask?"

"It's just that you don't seem to be very chatty."

"I'm sorry; maybe not being used to a woman telling me she loves me is, after all, bringing out the Englishness in me. Time for me to snap out of it."

With that, their conversation over the rest of the meal picked up, aided by a second bottle of wine.

Back in their hotel bedroom, George was uncertain what Isabel expected but she too was unsure of what George expected of her. She had never spent the night with a man before and, reminding herself that the best way to win George over would be by not being too forward, she did not want what she hoped would be their first night of many together to be one which would put him off her. Recognising some awkwardness on the part of Isabel, George reassured her by telling her that much as he was looking forward to spending the night with her this was just the start of a new stage of their relationship and he did not want either of them to wake up in the morning regretting what may have happened the night before.

George need not have worried; the travelling from London and the wine had tired both of them and not long after getting into bed they both nodded off to sleep. They both slept well and, with a train to Bayeux to catch, there was no time in the morning for anything more than cuddling up next to each other before making their way to Gare St-Lazare. During the train journey back to Bayeux, they spoke little of their night together, not least because there was little to talk about. Both agreed though on two things; the first was that Isabel's father was not to know and the second was that they should not waste any opportunities to spend more time together.

Back in Bayeux, Monsieur Laport was keen to know how their meetings in Paris had gone and, when told of the offers made to journalists to stay at the hotel, thoroughly approved. Monsieur Laport also had some news for them. Whilst they had been away, one of Monsieur Laport's uncles had passed away and as the uncle in question was a widower with no heirs following the death of his only child, a son, four years earlier at the Battle of the Somme, his chateau at Montfiquet some 15 kilometres away, had been left to Monsieur Laport. When asked what he planned to do with the chateau, Monsieur Laport said it was too early to decide but, as it would need looking after, he expected to move into it and live there. Believing this meant he expected Isabel to move with him, Isabel asked him what would happen to the house in Barbeville they were currently living in.

"Much as I would welcome George joining us in the new house, I think that may be asking too much of him. If he is agreeable to it, the house is available to him to live in."

Isabel's initial reaction was one of disappointment as she feared it would mean seeing less of George but, on reflection, she realised that, even if it did mean seeing less of George, it might also mean spending more time alone with George, with less constraint imposed upon how they behaved when in the presence of her father.

Business at the beginning of the new season was promising with bookings well up on the previous year but it was too early to tell if this pattern would continue through the summer months. Two of the journalists George and Isabel had met in Paris had taken up the offer to stay at the hotel and not long after favourable reports appeared in *Le Figaro* and *Le Petit Parisien*. By the end of the summer, bookings were up by more than twenty per cent on the previous year and many of the guests who had stayed at the hotel that summer re-booked for the following year.

Well before the end of summer, Monsieur Laport had moved into his new home in Montfiquet with Isabel but, whilst the hotel remained busy through the summer months, she stayed with George as often as she could. As with the previous year, Monsieur Laport decided that it did not make economic sense to keep the hotel open during the winter months and, as a result, Isabel had less reason to stay at the house in Barbeville with George than with her father. She still helped out with the running of the restaurant over the winter so she and George still saw plenty of each other but the more time that Isabel stayed with her father the more George missed her. This state of affairs seemed destined to continue until the hotel re-opened the following spring unless George or Isabel could come up with an alternative plan; much as they tried to think of one, the only one they thought would give Monsieur Laport no grounds to suspect some other motive was a trip to Paris again, ostensibly as part of their marketing plan to keep promoting the hotel business to its most likely customers. Monsieur Laport was agreeable to this but when Isabel suggested to George that they pay a second visit to London to see his family, George told her that whatever time they could spend away together he wanted to spend with just her; when Isabel heard this, she smiled to herself not just because it was flattering but also because she believed her policy of playing hard to get might just be working.

They embarked on their second trip to Paris in February, when restaurant bookings at the hotel were at their lowest. The plans for their trip were much the same as in the previous year, with them hosting a reception for existing customers and targeting the press. As they had not taken time off work for the best part of a year, they also wanted some of their time in Paris to themselves. Because of its central location, they returned to the same hotel they had stayed in before and, as with their previous visit, booked a double room.

The reception went well with Olivia putting on a good show, as she did with the journalists they met but she was keen to use her time in Paris alone with George without having to concern herself too much with hotel business. They spent the time they had to themselves walking along the banks of the Seine, wandering around Ile de la Cite and Ile St Louis and visiting the Pere Lachaise cemetery to pay their respects to Henri.

During their time in Paris, it became clear to Isabel that, even if she still had some doubts as to whether the less time they had spent together over the winter months had made George's heart grow fonder, she was in no doubt that such absences had made his desire for her much stronger. But Isabel was determined to resist him and made her position clear.

"You know I'm in love with you but I want to save myself for you for our wedding night."

George was somewhat taken back by this as, even if he knew she was in love with him, he had not given any serious thought to marrying her, not least because neither of them had ever broached the subject. In responding to her, he would have to choose his words carefully.

"Isabel, I totally respect what you're saying as I too would not want anything to happen between us which would jeopardise our relationship. We've not discussed marriage but perhaps now is as good a time as any to do so. I've not given it much thought, not because I'm not interested in marrying you but because I assumed that, if we wanted to be married to each other, we would both know when the time is right."

"Well George, maybe the right time is not far away as I feel I'm ready to marry you."

"This has all caught me rather by surprise, albeit a very welcome one. I just need a bit of time to think about it to convince myself it's the right thing for both of us. I promise you though that whatever my decision is, it will be the best for both of us. I respect you too much to do otherwise."

"I understand but, much as I love you, I won't wait for you for ever."

George knew he would have to make a decision as to whether he wanted to spend the rest of his life with Isabel. He had grown fonder of her the more time he spent with her and missed her when they were not together. There was little likelihood of him meeting anyone else in the foreseeable future but he needed to be certain that Isabel was the woman he wanted to marry and that he wanted to marry her not just for the sake of being able to make love to her.

Over the course of the next three weeks, George reasoned with himself and, playing devil's advocate, the only argument he could come up with for not marrying her was that he did not feel the same way as he had when he wanted to marry Olivia; although this was not a reason for not marrying Isabel, he did not want to feel, or for Isabel to feel, that he was only considering marriage to her because she had suggested it – he did not want to feel being pressurised into making a decision but instead wanted to feel that, if his decision was that he wanted to marry her, it was because that was what he wanted and that it was the right time to do so. Three weeks of humming and hawing over it was sufficient enough time for George to make up his mind. How he had felt with Olivia was never likely to be the same with anyone else but that was not good enough cause for him not to marry, or not to want to marry someone else. The fact that he had not thought of marriage before Isabel had suggested it was of no consequence – had the roles been reversed, he would not have expected Isabel to decline a proposal on the grounds she had not been the first of them to think of marriage. On a more positive note, there were plenty of good reasons for marrying her and, after three weeks, his mind was made up.

Having decided that he did want to marry Isabel after all, he was not sure if he should tell Isabel straightaway or whether he should only do so after seeking, and obtaining, Monsieur Laport's consent to their marriage. Having decided on the latter, he was keen to ensure that Isabel was not kept waiting too long before knowing of his intentions.

Needing to find the right moment to ask Monsieur Laport for Isabel's hand in marriage, the opportunity to ask presented itself early one evening over the Easter period. Although the hotel restaurant was busy over this period, Monsieur Laport had invited George to stay with him and Isabel at his new home and it was over a drink before dinner one evening whilst Isabel was preparing their supper that George chose to tackle the subject.

"Monsieur, I don't know if you've noticed but, even though we have tried not to show it in public, Isabel and I have become very attached to each other over the past two years. I don't think it has affected us at work other than for the better and I've now come to the conclusion that I'd like to spend the rest of my life with her. I recognise that this will only be possible if it has your full blessing and approval. I'm therefore, in a somewhat roundabout way, asking for your permission to marry her."

Monsieur Laport chose not to respond immediately as he thought to do so might suggest he had not given the matter sufficient time to consider his answer. After taking what seemed to George more than enough time, Monsieur Laport spoke.

"George, I can't say it has gone unnoticed how fond Isabel is of you – a father has an instinct for these things. And I can't say that I have for one moment disapproved of this. I, like Isabel, have come to admire and respect you and you've shown yourself to me to be exactly the sort of man I would want my daughter to marry. So I too, in my roundabout way, am saying that you have my unreserved permission to ask Isabel to be your wife."

"Monsieur Laport, I can't thank you enough. I intend to propose to her as soon as I catch her at the right moment and of course we'll let you know once that has happened."

It took George only three days to find the right moment. On the Tuesday after Easter, the restaurant was quieter than it had been over the Easter weekend; preparing for the evening bookings after the lunchtime guests had all gone had not taken long and George and Isabel had a couple of hours to kill before the first evening guests were expected.

As they were washing and changing for the evening, George knocked on the door to Isabel's bedroom and asked if he could come in for a moment. Once inside her room, he shut the door and came straight to the point.

"Isabel, when we were in Paris, you told me that you wanted to marry me and I asked you to allow me time to think about this. It has not taken me any time to know that I too want to marry you. I'm therefore asking if you will marry me."

"George, you know I want to marry you but before I say "yes", have you spoken to my father?"

"I have indeed asked for his permission and he has given it."

"In which case my answer is yes."

And with that she put her arms around George and kissed him.

"I promised your father that I would tell him once I had proposed to you so I'm keen that we tell him as soon as we can. I don't have an engagement ring for you yet because I want to choose one with you."

"That's fine although I'm sure I'd have been more than happy with anything you chose."

Before there was time to find a ring, George and Isabel announced their news to her father, which he had been expecting as he had given it his blessing. As well as having to find a ring, a date for the wedding had to be arranged and much as George and Isabel were keen to marry as soon as possible, George was equally keen that his parents be present at the wedding.

Once George heard back from his parents, he and Isabel settled on the church ceremony which they both wanted taking place on Saturday 10th September, with the requisite civil ceremony the day before, Monsieur Laport having urged them to wait until after the busy summer period was over.

The wedding planning went smoothly, the only contentious issue being whether to invite George's brother Edward and Olivia. Isabel argued that inviting them would show that George had forgiven them for what had happened and could now be put behind them although part of her wondered how George would feel if he saw Olivia again. George countered by answering that, if Olivia was not aware that he had survived the War, it might be better if she never knew and, if this was the case, better not to invite them. By way of compromise, they agreed that Edward and Olivia should only be invited if Olivia knew George had survived the War. George was tasked with asking his parents if either they or Edward had passed on to Olivia the news that George had indeed survived the War notwithstanding the presumption of his death; when his parents replied that neither they nor Edward had told Olivia that the presumption of George's death was a false one, Isabel wondered why but accepted that Edward and Olivia were to be excluded from the guest list.

George was delighted his parents were able to make the journey to France to attend his wedding; the absence of Edward who would, in other circumstances, have been his best man, meant George decided not to ask anyone else to fulfil that role. The civil marriage ceremony was a formal occasion with the real celebrations taking place a day later after the service held in the church in Montfiquet. They took off the week following their wedding for their honeymoon; tempted as they were to spend it in Paris, they chose instead the fashionable resort of Deauville where, true to her word, Isabel no longer had cause to put up any resistance to George's advances.

Once back at work, Isabel returned to her old home in Barbeville to live with George. Having spent so much time together for the best part of three years before their wedding, the two of them settled easily into married life. Each knew what to expect of the other so neither found they had to make adjustments to their lifestyle to accommodate the other. In many ways, being married to each other changed little but, in other ways, it brought them closer together, a togetherness which only grew when Isabel announced just after their first anniversary that she was pregnant.

Isabel was able to reduce her workload during the first months of her pregnancy as business at the hotel quietened down over the winter months but, by the time the hotel was back to full capacity the following spring, her condition forced her to slow things down. She gave birth to a son in June 1923 and much as she and George were thrilled to have produced an heir, the birth was not without complications. Damage to her fallopian tubes during the birth meant not only that it took Isabel the best part of six months to feel over the worst but also that her chances of being able to produce a sibling for her newborn more unlikely than not.

Part 6

1923-1944

George and Isabel proved to be doting parents and, rather than being disappointed at being unable to produce another child, were thankful that their one and only child was healthy. Agreeing to name their baby Paul Henri was straightforward as they wanted one of his given names to be one which was spelt, even if not pronounced, the same in French and English and the other to be in memory of Isabel's brother and without whom George and Isabel would never have met.

Despite more and more of Isabel's time being taken up looking after Paul, the hotel business continued to prosper throughout the 1920s helped by a buoyant French economy; over the summer months, the hotel was booked to capacity and over the winter months, the hotel's restaurant was always busy as it continued to provide the best meal in the vicinity. George and Isabel had a more than comfortable lifestyle, one with which they could not be more content. The 1930s brought different challenges with Paris hit by the Great Depression in 1931, which saw many of the hotel's more affluent Parisian clients choosing to stay at home over the summer period. Events in neighbouring countries were, in George's opinion, more cause for concern, with Germany becoming a Nazi state with Hitler as chancellor and with the

Civil War in Spain. The annexation by Germany first of Austria and then of the Sudetanland part of Czechoslovakia in 1938 and the subsequent invasion of the rest of Czechoslovakia in early 1939 were of grave concern, causing George to question whether he and his family should move to another country. Isabel was certain Hitler would not send his troops into France but George was less convinced.

"The Nazi tyrant continues to break his promises so what's to stop him invading the Alsace-Lorraine which no doubt he thinks belongs to Germany anyway?"

"Our politicians won't let him."

"What've they got to stop him? D'you think the French have sufficient resources to put up a fight and, even if they have, are they enough to deter him? And d'you think that, after all the losses suffered in the last War, they'd be willing to fight again? I'm not so sure."

George did at least persuade her that it made good sense to have in place a plan should Germany invade France. They could either stay put or move abroad but, if they were to move abroad, the choices open to them were limited; they ruled out moving to Spain as it was seen as being sympathetic to the Nazi cause, leaving them to choose between Britain, Switzerland, Portugal or away from Europe altogether. Isabel ruled out another continent because she did not want to be too far away from her father and, whilst George was reluctant to return to live in Britain, this was the most logical choice.

Although George and Isabel had in place a plan to move back to England if they felt it necessary, they were less clear about when they would need to implement it. Isabel was reluctant to move there before it was absolutely essential because she did not want to abandon her father but, if they left it until the last minute, there was no guarantee that they would be able to get away. They both agreed though they would be willing to leave, and ready to, at a moment's notice if need be.

As George predicted, Hitler's sights were not just limited to Austria and Czechoslovakia, despite the assurances he had given to British and French politicians. The invasion of Poland led to France declaring war against Germany in early September 1939 but, despite its declaration of war, there was no imminent requirement for its armed forces to take any action against Germany. That all changed though in May 1940 when Germany invaded the Low Countries of Belgium, Luxembourg and The Netherlands.

Although there was no doubt in his mind that Germany would not stop at the Low Countries, with France most likely to be the next target, George was unable to persuade Isabel to flee until after Paris fell to the Germans in June 1940. Reluctant as she was to leave her home, she accepted that she had agreed with George that they would head for England if Germany invaded France and, as that had now happened, they should make their way to England without delay. What neither of them had foreseen though was Paul's unwillingness to join them. Paul had had his seventeenth birthday the day Paris fell and he felt it was his duty to stay behind and fight the Germans rather than risk being branded a coward. Much as George tried to reason with him that his safety could not be guaranteed if he stayed behind and lived under German occupation, Paul was willing to take the risk in the belief that ultimately Germany could not win the War and resistance in the meantime was better conducted from within than from afar. Paul's refusal to join his parents in England made Isabel question George if it was right for them to go and after much debate, they agreed they would not leave unless Paul was willing to join them. It was only a matter of days though before the decision was taken out of their hands as the Germans moved west of Paris, taking control not just of Bayeux but also Cherbourg, the port from which they had planned to make their escape.

Although leaving via Cherbourg was no longer an option, George was still keen to move to an area not occupied by the Germans but Isabel refused to move unless they could also persuade Paul to move with them. Living under the Germans presented a greater risk for George than for Isabel and Paul because of his British nationality and, although his papers showed that he had French citizenship, he knew it would be all too easy for the Germans to find out about his British background. Paul though would not budge on his determination to stay and fight, leaving Isabel to decide between her husband and her son. She was fully aware that, by staying behind, they would be putting themselves in greater danger but she questioned whether they would be any better off moving to England if, as now seemed likely, Germany would invade Britain also. Leaving Paul behind would cause her to worry non-stop about him and, on balance, she would prefer to know about his safety even if that involved the inevitable hardships of living under German rule.

George came to the conclusion that he had a difficult choice to make - he could either stay in France with his family with all the dangers associated with that or he could try to flee, leaving his wife and son behind. Like Isabel, if he left Isabel and Paul behind, he would worry more about their wellbeing than if he was still with them.

Trapped by his predicament, he was disappointed that Isabel had gone back on what they had agreed but he understood why and bore her no grudge for not keeping to her word. Ultimately his decision boiled down to whether he wanted to stay with Isabel or leave without her, a decision that, despite the risks involved, was an easy one to make; in no circumstances was he going to leave without her and they would just have to get by as best they could living under the Germans.

The German occupation saw Isabel's father return to live with his daughter, son-in-law and grandson as the Germans requisitioned his home in Montfiquet making it their headquarters from which to command forces controlling the coast nearby. This was not the only inconvenience caused by the occupation as the locals found that, as well as their freedom of movement being restricted by the imposition of curfews upon them, they also had to put up with food shortages caused by feeding the extra mouths of the invaders.

It took George and Isabel no time to realise that occupation by the Germans would put an end to tourism and, as most of the hotel's guests up until then had been tourists, keeping the hotel business open was no longer a viable proposition. They decided to close the hotel business until further notice but agreed to keep the hotel bar and restaurant open for business for the time being, acknowledging though that even this business would inevitably suffer unless they were willing to serve the unwelcome intruders.

Initially, they were unwilling to serve Germans but their refusal to do so prompted a visit from a German officer who had been ordered to look into the matter; during the visit, it was made clear to George that if he chose to continue not serving German customers, not only did he risk being forced to close the hotel down altogether but he also risked being sent away to a labour camp. He knew that the consequences of being forced to serve Germans would be the loss of his local clientele but that seemed a more attractive fate than a labour camp, even if serving Germans might be seen by some of the locals as collaboration.

He decided that he had no choice but to allow German soldiers based in the area to use the bar and restaurant as and when they chose, a decision which predictably saw the locals choosing to take their custom elsewhere.

The bar became a popular watering hole for the Germans despite George and the hotel staff making no effort to make them feel welcome. Over time, locals started to return to the bar; initially the locals who started frequenting the bar were French women consorting with the German troops and, once word got around that this was happening, occasional visits were paid by some of the local men. It was Paul who pointed out to his father why this was happening – the men were there to make a note of which of their female compatriots were "collaborating" with the enemy.

In the summer of 1942, German activity in the area increased following Hitler's directive for the construction of the Atlantic Wall, which involved reinforcing defensive positions at a number of locations along France's Atlantic coastline. In the area close to

Bayeux, eleven new German battery stations were built along a twenty-seven mile stretch of coast line.

One evening as he was closing the hotel bar for the night, not long after the construction of the new battery stations had been completed, George was approached by the last customer to leave, a Frenchmen who had been sitting on his own in the corner of the bar.

"Monsieur Hart, I shall be brief and I do not need your answer straightaway as I recognise you might need time to think about it. I am aware that a number of German soldiers frequent your bar and therefore you may overhear things which may be of interest to others like myself. I and my colleagues are keen to receive any information which may assist us in, shall we say, making life uncomfortable for our unwanted visitors. Are you willing to help us?"

George could not be certain whether or not the person who had approached him was working as an undercover agent so, before giving an answer, asked who he was.

"Monsieur, I've not seen you in my bar before. You clearly know who I am but, as yours is not a familiar face, would you kindly introduce yourself?"

"Monsieur Hart, you don't need to know who I am; all you need know is that I'm a loyal Frenchman working with the Resistance."

"How can I know that? How can you prove that you are not, like so many of our compatriots, working with the Germans?"

"I'm not sure I can prove it to you. But I can tell you that we know that you're not really a Frenchman, that you're English. If I was working with the Germans, don't you think, by now, they would know of your background and have had you arrested?"

"Give me a couple of days to mull it over."

"That's fine; I or one of my colleagues will make contact with you in a couple of days."

"If it's one of your colleagues, how will I know?"

"He or she will introduce himself or herself by saying something which will leave you in no doubt that he or she is not working for the Germans."

The Frenchman departed leaving George to reflect on what had been asked of him.

Once again he found himself having to make a decision he would have preferred not to have to make. He told Isabel what had happened and that he would not agree to pass on information as requested if she was opposed to the idea.

"George, we're living in times when we all have to make decisions we would rather not have to make. Work out the advantages and disadvantages. Then choose which decision on balance you prefer to live with. Only you can make that decision but I'll support you in whichever decision you make."

The obvious benefit of providing information was the prospect of it helping the fight against the Germans but with that would come a greater risk of being caught and having to suffer the consequences; such consequences would at best be imprisonment and at worst being shot. By not providing information, the risk of imprisonment and the possibility of being shot would be less, but George would not only have to live with his own conscience for failing to assist in the war effort against the Germans but also the reaction of those who would see the refusal to assist as cowardice or, even worse, collaboration. George was well aware that the only reason he and Isabel were still in France and not in Britain was because their son had wanted to stay behind and fight. He realised that, if his decision was not to assist, it could well be his own son who would view this as cowardice, a situation so repugnant that the decision was an easy one for him to make.

George waited to be contacted, not knowing who would make the contact and not entirely sure he would know when it was being made. It came two days after he had first been approached and came from a source he had not anticipated, the source being his son Paul. Although Paul was still living with his parents, with the downturn in business at the hotel, there was no longer enough work to justify employing him there and, as a consequence, he took a job working as an engineer in an aeronautical components factory nearby. It had been the idea of the French Resistance that he be employed at the factory which had been taken over by the Germans, to allow him to report on the specifications of the aircraft being manufactured there and, if the right opportunity arose, to sabotage production.

"Papa, I know you've been expecting to hear from someone who'll say something which will make it clear to you that he or she isn't working for the Germans. I'm hoping that, by my saying that, you'll recognise that I'm the contact."

"So Paul, you're the contact, are you? I wasn't expecting that."

"Yes, papa, I am and the reason is because my talking to you will appear less suspicious than a stranger talking to you. Are you able to tell me your decision?"

"Yes, I can. I am willing to help and pass on any information I hear which I think may be of interest."

"Excellent, papa. I shall pass this on. We'll have to work out a system which will allow you to pass on information discreetly. I wasn't sure you would agree to assist but was hopeful you would and I'm very proud of you."

Much as Paul wanted to hug his father for agreeing to help, he thought better of it in case it looked unusual enough behaviour to arouse suspicion in anyone watching.

It was another week before Paul explained to his father how information was to be passed on. George's only contact was to be Paul as it would give the Germans less reason to question why they were conversing with each other. By agreeing to go along with this arrangement, George was concerned he was making Paul take unnecessary risks but Paul would have none of this.

"Papa, it's only because of me that you're here in France living under German occupation. I'll always be indebted to you for that and I'll do everything in my power to ensure that no one will be able to trace back to you that you're the source of information I pass on."

Having agreed to help, George knew that, to be of any use, he would have to eavesdrop more if he was to pick up any bits of helpful information, but in a subtle way. Having previously tried to avoid engaging in conversation with German customers, he no longer could do so but changes in the way he treated his customers would have to be unrecognisable.

His first attempts at listening in on discussions at his bar were somewhat fruitless, with most of the customers' conversations he overheard being of a more private nature; anything said about the war effort tended to be no more than idle gossip. By early 1943, George noticed that his bar was attracting more and more custom from Frenchmen and passed this on to Paul. Although he expected this piece of information to be of little interest, it proved to be very useful as it alerted the Resistance to the presence in the area of members of the Milice, the French paramilitary organisation working with the Germans. Their presence in the area was as unwelcome as that of the Germans as their cruel treatment of captured Resistance fighters matched that of the Gestapo.

Identifying who they were though was far from easy; they were native Frenchmen from all walks of life who understood local customs and dialects and had no difficulty in blending in with and being mistaken for locals, who by and large wanted to keep themselves to themselves. With the Milice waging war on the Resistance, their members in turn were primary targets for the Resistance, not just because they were viewed as traitors but also in the belief the likely reprisals for killing members of the Milice would be less severe than any reprisals from the Germans should German soldiers be killed.

Knowing members of the Milice were in the area, Paul told his father that the Resistance was keen to hear more than just bits of information that might be overheard; they needed George to help identify Milice members. The Resistance had reason to believe the hotel bar was a meeting place for them, so George was asked to keep an eye out for any new customers and point them out to Paul. Paul also warned his father that the Milice were after informants, so George would need to be particularly vigilant.

George had to go about his information-gathering role discreetly; he could not appear too eager to engage in conversation but he was unlikely to be of any help to the Resistance without doing so to some degree. Over time, he acquired a certain instinct for recognising members of the Milice and distinguishing them from those working with the Resistance; those working for the Milice tended to be more raucous after a couple of drinks, perhaps because they felt they had nothing to hide from the German soldiers present.

George was never party to what the Resistance would do with the information he passed on but one evening late in 1943, Paul came to the bar and warned him to keep well away from the entrance to the hotel as his customers were leaving that evening. George knew better than to ask why and simply heeded the advice. Not more than three minutes after the last customers left, George could hear shooting in the street outside. The shooting lasted no more than two minutes and, at the end of it, four Frenchmen were lying dead in the streets; no German soldiers had been killed and no one was left in any doubt that the Milice had been targeted. Reprisals were swift and although no German soldiers had been shot, the German authorities in command were keen to exact retribution; two days after the shooting, eight local men were rounded up and shot in the main square in Bayeux.

As well as the shooting of men randomly chosen, others were arrested and questioned about the incident. Included amongst those questioned were George and Paul but both were released without their interrogators resorting to torture. In the case of Paul, he was released after he explained that he worked at the nearby aeronautical components factory and, since the factory was now used to help build parts for German aircraft, he was helping the German cause, an explanation which was verified by those in charge at the factory. In the case of George, those interrogating him needed more convincing of his innocence as they assumed the signal to start the shooting would have come from within the hotel when those killed were leaving the bar – the intervention of senior German officers who were regular customers at the bar was enough to persuade those interrogating George that any further questioning of George would not lead them to the real culprits.

The severity of the reprisals shocked the locals but left them in no doubt as to how similar acts of sabotage would be treated. In the short term, the killing of eight locals regardless of their culpability, had, as far as the Germans were concerned, the desired effect as the Resistance seemed to go to ground but the Germans were aware that this was unlikely to last and, instead of discouraging further acts of sabotage, made the Resistance more determined to retaliate. It was just a matter of time.

As far as George was concerned, he knew he had had a lucky escape and he told Paul that he was not sure he still had the stomach to be an informant, passing on information which he thought would only ever be of limited value. Although Paul could understand his father's reluctance to continue to be an informant, he reassured his father that he had played a vital role in highlighting the presence of Milice members in the area. Information about those siding with the Germans had been of great value to those still willing to fight them.

Over the next couple of months, with George trying to be more discreet, there was nothing for him to pass on to Paul. One evening in April 1944, when passing on that he had nothing to report, he was asked by Paul if he had heard anything about additional forces being sent to the area. Paul did not explain why he wanted to know save to say that it was widely known that Hitler feared an attack from across the English Channel and, although no one could be certain where and when such an attack would take place, it was important to know whether or not Hitler was sending reinforcements to strengthen the German positions in any particular areas along the coast. George promised to keep an ear to the ground and report if he heard anything about the bolstering up defences in the region.

Paul visited his father on a frequent basis to see if his father had any news to pass on, but all George could report was that he had not heard any talk about more troops arriving in the area. Little did George know this was exactly what Paul and his Resistance colleagues wanted to hear.

On a visit to his father in early June, Paul told his father that there were rumours that there was likely to be a serious aerial attack in the area within the next couple of days and was warning him that he, Isabel and Isabel's father would need to be somewhere safe during the attack. Although Paul knew that a large scale attack was imminent, he did not pass this on as it was vital that only those that needed to know were aware of Operation Overlord, the operation involving the landings of Allied troops on five nearby beaches. On being told this, George was concerned not only for his own safety and that of Isabel and her father but also that of Paul.

"Where will you be when the attack is launched?"

"I don't know but there will work which will need to be done at ground level to minimise counter-attacks."

"You won't be taking any unnecessary risks, will you?"

"I don't intend to but, whilst the Nazis are still here, no one is safe. We must all do what we can to be rid of them."

Following Paul's warning, George, Isabel and her father decided it would be safer to stay at the hotel where they would have access to its cellar which would offer them better protection from an aerial raid, rather than at their home nearby. Not long after midnight in the early hours of 6th June, they were woken by the noise of bombing in the distance followed by the noise of aircraft overhead. The noise was a cue for them to retreat to the cellar for the rest of the night. The noise from above was such that it made sleep impossible.

George ventured upstairs as dawn was breaking. Although he could hear the sound of guns in the distance, it was only when he looked out from the top floor of the hotel that he could sense what was going on. From what he could see, the overnight attack had not affected Bayeux but he was in no doubt that a major battle was underway along the coastline less than 10 miles away and that, if those attacking were able to break through the German coastal defences, Bayeux could well be their next target.

Much as he wanted to find somewhere safer for Isabel and her father, staying put was as good an option as any and they had little choice but to keep their heads down until the battle was won, how ever long that might take. As George peered out from the top of the hotel, he was not to know that, before he and Isabel had finished breakfast that morning, the Allied troops were already scouting the outskirts of Bayeux less than two miles from its centre.

Having resigned themselves to seeing out the battle raging overhead in a cellar, excursions to the floors above were kept to a minimum. Isabel tried to make the cellar as comfortable as she could but there were limits to how comfortable she could make it and they all realised that, if they were going to have to spend much time down there, no good would come from complaining about it.

During his trip upstairs to the hotel kitchen to find some food for lunch, George took the opportunity to look outside to survey the situation. Despite the continuous noise of gunfire, there did not seem to be any fighting in the streets; what he did notice though was German troops on the move as if they were being posted elsewhere. By nightfall, the streets of Bayeux were quiet. George assumed the movement of troops to their new postings had been completed but the silence in the streets was not enough to tempt him to venture outside. Instead he braced himself for another night underground.

The scenes outside first thing the following morning were much the same as the previous evening, with no sign of any German troops. That changed later that morning when, instead of German troops patrolling the streets, Allied troops were. When George first spotted the armoured vehicles of the Allies outside, he was anxious to know what was going on. The vehicles were not stopping but soon word spread that the city had been liberated with little bloodshed as the Germans had abandoned the city to provide reinforcements on the Cherbourg peninsula. There were rumours that German snipers were still in the city but many locals ignored the advice to stay indoors as they celebrated freedom and forced George to re-open the hotel bar so that they could toast the liberation of their city.

Included amongst those celebrating was Paul, who explained to his father what had been happening over the past couple of days. Unknown to George, the Allied forces had launched their attack on the beaches nearby; the attack had taken Hitler by surprise as he was convinced any such attack would be launched further up the coast nearer to Calais. Paul told his father that the small part played by him was nevertheless an important one as, had his father heard that the Germans were sending reinforcements to bolster the defences around the Normandy beaches and passed this information on, the attack would at best have cost many more lives and at worst been put off altogether. The fact that such information had not been passed on by George helped the powers that be decide that the attack should go ahead on the Normandy beaches as planned. Paul warned his father that the fact that Bayeux had been liberated so quickly did not mean the Germans were not putting up a better fight in the other towns and cities in the vicinity. Intercepted wireless messages had put Paul and his colleagues on notice that German forces were headed for Normandy to counter the Allied advances and it was up to them to do what they could to prevent or stall this.

Relieved as he was that Bayeux had escaped the worst of the fighting, George was concerned for Paul's safety. His determination to fight left George in no doubt that Paul would be taking risks endangering his life. Over the next few days, news spread that the German resistance in the area was at breaking point, not helped by the delays in reinforcements getting through, with the work of the French Resistance fighters, amongst whom was Paul, playing a major role in causing such delays.

Although they were able to gain control of Bayeux within two days after landing on the beaches nearby, the Allied troops came up against much stronger resistance as they headed east towards the city of Caen, less than twenty miles away. It was another month before they gained control of that part of the city lying to the west of the River Orme which flowed through its centre and a further six weeks before the Germans retreated from the city, opening up the way to Paris for the Allied forces.

Whilst the battle for Caen was raging, Paul was working with other Resistance fighters to the south of Caen. They were tasked with cutting down trees to block roads with the aim of holding up the arrival of German troops from the south and then ambushing them as they attempted to clear the fallen trees from the roads. Although such missions were considered high-risk, the Resistance fighters usually retreated from their firing positions immediately after the initial burst, before the Germans were in a position to fire back, confident the Germans would not pursue them as they retreated.

It was whilst retreating after his second such mission that Paul and his colleagues found themselves under fire from members of the Milice, on the receiving end of an ambush in much the same way as their German targets had been only minutes earlier. That they had been betrayed was beyond doubt but much as they knew they had been let down by an infiltrator, they had no time to dwell on that as their priority was survival. The Milice were experienced in warfare and had chosen as their point of ambush a position not only one from which they could not easily be seen but one which left those they were firing at most exposed. The first shots fired by the Milice hit two of Paul's colleagues but, as they lay there injured in the firing line, any attempt to help them would have led to more of Paul's colleagues being hit.

Paul's first reaction to being fired at was to fall to the ground and look around to see if he could see where the shots were coming from but whoever was firing at them had good cover. Paul could not just lie where he was and needed to find better cover. During a lull in the shooting, he made a dash for the nearest trees only to feel an excruciating pain in his left leg just before he reached them. Despite being hit, Paul was able to stumble his way to the cover the trees provided and from where he was able to inspect the seriousness of his wound.

He had been hit in the leg, above the knee. Needing to do something to stop the bleeding, he tore off the trouser leg of the leg which had been hit and used it as a tourniquet, tying it as tightly as he could above the wound. Even though he was no longer in the line of fire, he knew he needed to get away as far as he could, fearing that the Milice would be intent on killing Paul and those of his colleagues not already dead, so that there were no witnesses to their betrayal. Unable to use his wounded leg, Paul started crawling his way further into the wooded area around him; he felt guilty about abandoning his colleagues but reckoned that, in his condition, he would be of no help to them. He did not know how long he had been crawling when he noticed the shooting had stopped. Nor did he know why the shooting had stopped – he wondered whether it was because his colleagues had all been killed but, whatever the reason, he had to keep moving even if he had little idea where he was heading.

Once the shooting had stopped, Paul looked around for a fallen branch which could support his weight, knowing that he would move more quickly using a branch as a crutch. It took a few try-outs before he found a suitable one and even though his leg was still causing him considerable pain, the crutch allowed him to move at a better pace. Paul stayed amongst the trees for as long as he could before coming to a clearing in the forest. At the far side of the clearing, less than four hundred yards away, he spotted a labourer's cottage and, knowing that he needed treatment urgently, had no choice but to head for it in the hope someone would be there who could help him.

By the time he reached the cottage, he was exhausted and barely able to stand. Hearing noises from inside he knocked on what appeared to be the cottage's only entrance. Before the door was opened, Paul noticed the occupant peering through one of the ground floor windows at him. A minute later the front door was opened.

"What d'you want?" Paul was asked in a tone which was decidedly unwelcome.

"I've been shot in the leg and need help; can you help me?"

"How can I help you?" Again the tone was such that, even if help could be provided, it would not be forthcoming.

"I'm not sure how near you are to the nearest town but I need to get to a doctor or a hospital."

"Who shot you?"

Paul knew his answer to this question could determine whether or not the cottage's occupant, who Paul took to be a gamekeeper, would provide any help. If Paul were to tell him he had been shot by the Milice and he was sympathetic to its cause, Paul could not expect any help. He could not afford to take this risk.

"I was on a road near Caen when a German patrol passing by was fired upon. I was caught in the crossfire and don't know who hit me."

This seemed to appease his interrogator.

"The nearest hospital is about four miles away in Caen. I'll see if I can get you there. You'll have to lie in the back of my cart."

"Thank you. How soon can you get me there?"

"Not 'til the morning. It's too late in the day to get there and back in daylight."

It had already dawned on Paul that his means of transport to hospital would be by horse and cart and there was nothing he could do about it. He had an uncomfortable night sleeping in a chair with his wounded leg rested on another chair. He had not been able to stem the loss of blood nor had the pain gone and as a consequence, he felt much weaker when he woke the following morning. The early morning light allowed the two of them to set off on the journey to Caen first thing, with Paul lying down on some empty sacks left in the cart. The journey was slow and Paul felt every bump as the cart made its way along various dirt tracks before reaching smoother surfaces. By the time they reached the hospital, Paul was a delirious state, the loss of blood, the pain and the lack of sleep affecting not only his physical condition but his mental one as well. The gamekeeper left Paul in the cart as he made his way to the hospital entrance. Once inside, he spoke to the first nurse he saw and explained that he had a badly injured man in the back of his cart who needed to be stretchered into the hospital. With the fighting still going on all around Caen, the hospital staff was being over-worked coping with military as well as civilian casualties but the nurse agreed to come and see what condition Paul was in. After seeing him, she told the gamekeeper that she would be back as soon as she could be but that it might be as much as thirty minutes before stretcher-bearers would be with them. Much as he wanted to get back to his cottage as soon as he could, the gamekeeper stayed with Paul until help arrived.

Paul was barely conscious when the stretcher arrived to transfer him from the back of the cart to the hospital. Once Paul had been lifted on to the stretcher, the gamekeeper said to one of the stretcher-bearers before heading back that Paul had appeared at his cottage the previous afternoon and had told him that he had been shot by German soldiers.

As soon as Paul was admitted to the hospital, he was seen by a doctor. The doctor was concerned that the wound to Paul's leg had become infected. His first priority was to clean and dress the wound to try and prevent the infection spreading.

Despite the efforts of the medics at the hospital, Paul's condition deteriorated as he slipped in and out of consciousness. The doctors feared for the worst and during Paul's second night there, they were unable to resuscitate him. Much as his death was a terrible loss, it just one of numerous tragedies the hospital was having to deal with.

Having arrived at the hospital without any means of identification and with the gamekeeper being unable to tell the hospital staff who Paul was, no one at the hospital knew who to notify of his death. His body was taken to the hospital mortuary where it would remain until someone could identify him, failing which it would be taken to the city cemetery for burial.

Whilst Paul was at the hospital, George was visited by a young man who introduced himself as Claude.

"Monsieur Hart, I was wondering if you have heard from Paul recently."

"No, I haven't heard from him for a few days. Why do you ask?"

"Monsieur, I was with Paul three days ago when we were ambushed by members of the Milice on our way back from a sortie. The last I saw of Paul was him crawling away having been shot in the leg. I haven't been back there since so don't know if he got away safely."

"Where was this?"

"We were on the outskirts of Caen, to the south of the city. Judging by how Paul was moving, I think he was in need of urgent medical help. I can only presume that, if you haven't seen him, he made his way to a doctor or hospital; if not, I fear for his wellbeing."

"Have you checked with any of the hospitals to see if he has been admitted to any of them?"

"No. I think we may need to."

"Claude, what sort of sortie were you and Paul on?"

"Monsieur, I can't tell you exactly but I can tell you that it was for a good cause."

George told Isabel about the visit from Claude before setting off in search of Paul at nearby hospitals. Although he thought it unlikely Paul was at the hospital in Bayeux, he went there first but had no joy. He then headed to Caen. Having a good idea which hospital in Caen was the most likely one to have admitted Paul, George chose that one to visit first. On entering the hospital, George explained why he was there, asking whether a young man with the name of Paul Hart and an injured leg had been admitted. George was told that no one with that name had been admitted but, with the number of military men being admitted to the hospital, there were many patients whose names were not known.

As George was on his way out of the hospital, a nurse approached him.

"Monsieur, I overheard a bit of your conversation. I understand you are looking for a young man with leg injuries. We admitted someone to hospital with a leg wound three days ago but no one knew who he was, not even the farm labourer who brought him here. Perhaps that is the person you are looking for."

"Is it possible for me to see if it's him?"

"Let me see if I can arrange it. Please wait a moment."

When the nurse returned, she told George that he could see the young man in question, before adding that he must be prepared for some bad news because, if it was Paul, he had sadly passed away the day before. The nurse escorted him to the hospital mortuary where the mortician took him to the body; he stood still fearing the worst as the sheet covering the body was pulled back to reveal Paul. He took a while to compose himself before leaning over the body to kiss his dead son on his forehead before leaving. The nurse was waiting outside and knew without having to say anything that the dead man was George's son.

"I'm so sorry; we tried everything we could to save him but his wound was such that he must have shown great courage to survive as long as he did."

"I can only thank you for your efforts."

The shock of seeing his son lying there left George unable to think of anything else to say. He was dreading having to break the terrible news to Isabel and it was only when he was making his way back home that he realised that he would have to make arrangements to bury Paul.

Paul's funeral took place in Bayeux seven days after Paul had passed away. It was attended by a number of locals who were not known to George or Isabel. Amongst those present was Claude and, as the mourners were leaving, Claude approached George.

"Monsieur, I cannot express how sorry I am for you and your wife. Paul was a heroic, patriotic Frenchman and you can be proud of the contribution he made to the liberation of Normandy. Now is not the time to tell you but one day, when the War is over and France has rid itself of Nazis, I'll tell you about his heroic exploits."

"Thank you. It is comforting to hear that his death may not have been entirely in vain, although that is not how it currently feels. Perhaps over time we'll be able to come to terms with it better than we can now and maybe then I'll be more understanding of the sacrifice he has made."

The death of her only son was not something Isabel ever came to terms with; to her, no sacrifice justified such a loss. Although he too felt Paul's loss as much as Isabel, George coped better with their one and only child having been taken from them. It took more than a year before he felt able to speak to Claude about Paul, what he had been up to before his death and what had had happened on the day he was shot. When he knew, much as he wanted to share it with Isabel, he never felt able to as there was never a moment when he thought she would be emotionally strong enough to hear it.

Hearing what Claude had told him about Paul made George immensely proud of his son and his commitment to trying to free France from German rule. The good cause for which Paul was fighting and the contribution he made to France regaining control of its own land would never be adequate compensation for the loss of his life but it was at least some comfort to George, a comfort which many other families, who suffered the loss of loved ones for no reason at all other than the bigotry and cruelty of their enemies, were deprived of.

As 1944 drew to a close, it was a time of mixed emotions for George. He looked forward to re-opening the hotel but his life would be less purposeful without Paul. Life too with Isabel would never quite be the same again - the loss of Paul caused her to be more withdrawn, no more having the same *joie de vivre* or sparkle that she had had in the early years of their marriage.

Part 7

1944-1979

Much as France celebrated its liberation from German rule, it took time before life was back to normal. Everyone seemed to have someone to hate or resent. As soon as the Germans had been ejected from France, the Communists assumed control, in the belief that the lifestyle on offer in Russia was a better option. Such a choice ignored the possibility of Russia invading France in the same way as the Germans had and was more or less an open invitation for such an invasion. It took no more than a week for the Communists to be ousted but, even in such a short time, they allowed their political ideals to cause unnecessary havoc as privately-owned assets were sequestrated and anyone accused of collaborating with the Nazis slung into prison without a fair trial.

Patriotic Frenchmen despised the way so many of their compatriots had stood back helplessly allowing the enemy to take over without a fight or, even worse, had sided with them. In particular, those French women and girls who had consorted so freely, openly and willingly with German troops were the target of much of the hate. Others resented the fact that Britain and the Commonwealth, along with America, had come to France's rescue for the second time in a little over a quarter of a century, too proud to accept that France had been unable to do this on its own.

For many, they were never able to overcome these prejudices but, for George, his only bitterness was towards the Milice.

It took eleven months after the liberation of Bayeux for the War to finally come to an end. Only then could George turn his attention to re-opening the hotel but, as with the re-opening after the end of the First World War, it would take time to build up the clientele.

Not long after the German surrender, a letter arrived for George and, although the handwriting on the envelope was a bit shaky, he immediately recognised it as his father's. He had received no news from his parents for nearly six years and, knowing how much those living in London had suffered in the War, he tore open the envelope with some trepidation. The beginning of the letter was not what George was expecting to read as it opened with his father writing that he did not know if George was still alive to receive the letter and that, if he wasn't, perhaps the reader could reply to let him know. George's father then wrote that clearly he hoped and prayed that this was not the case and that the reader was indeed his son. After this somewhat unexpected start to the letter, its contents then became more newsy, with George's father passing on the sad news that Edward has been killed whilst at work during the Blitz and George's mother had died only weeks later after suffering a heart attack, no doubt brought on by Edward's death.

Despite not having seen his brother for nearly thirty years and little of his mother over the same period, George was very saddened to hear of their deaths. He also felt particularly sorry for his father who would have to cope with life on his own, with those closest to him no longer being there for him. George knew it was now his responsibility to make as much effort as possible to spend time with his father and hoped that, in his retirement, his father would find it easier to spend longer with Isabel and him in France.

Writing back to his father, he knew that he also had to break the news about Paul. Even though it had been four years since the deaths of his mother and brother and even though the Harts were just one of so many families that had suffered a similar fate, his father was shocked to hear of another loss within his family, especially that of Paul, its youngest member.

Keen as they were to see each other, the best time to meet again would be over the Christmas period. With the hotel business making it difficult for George to take too much time off work, his father agreed that he should make the trip to France.

Spending Christmas together made both George and his father appreciate the need to see more of each other. His father was already in his seventies and even though he was in good health, neither knew how much longer this would last and with George fully committed to managing the hotel, for how much longer his father would be able to make the journey to France. They had discussed the idea of his father moving to France but his father was reluctant to make such a move.

Time with his father made George realise how little time they had spent together. With time away at boarding school and university and time as a prisoner-of-war, followed by his self-imposed exile, too much time with his father had already been lost and George was keen to make up for it before it was too late.

Over the next seven years, the two of them saw more of each other than had been the case for the previous fifty years but, as George's father approached eighty, his health started to deteriorate. Recognising that each time together could be the last, George's father was keen to pass on his family history before it was too late. Being the only surviving son and having lost his own son, George wondered why his father was keen to pass this on as, once George died, it would be of no interest to anyone.

His father explained.

"George, first I think it's important that everyone knows about their family background; it's what I think of as your own history. Anyone can read about history in books but there's nothing personal about that; one's own family history is personal and usually much more fascinating.

That brings me on to the second reason I'm keen for you to know about our family history. One subject we've never talked about because of what happened is Edward's family and, as we've never discussed it, you may be unaware that you're not the last in the line of Harts. Olivia and Edward had a daughter who is still alive, as indeed is Olivia. Their daughter Jill recently gave birth to a son who they have named Walter. I'd hate to think that when Walter grows up, he knows nothing of his ancestry and there's no one to tell him."

This all came as somewhat of a surprise to George, not least hearing his father mention Olivia's name. "Father, hearing you tell me about our family means a huge amount to me and I understand why it's important to you to know that Walter too will know about his family background. But surely, whilst you still have time, you can record it for him or tell his mother."

"That is indeed true; but I was hoping that, by telling you, it might mend bridges. You could use the information I pass on to you as a reason to contact the one or two living relations you do have."

"Much as I'd like to fulfil your hopes, whilst Olivia is still alive it's not that simple. If I contact her daughter, I can't expect her not to tell Olivia and, if Olivia were to be told I had survived the first War, I don't know how she would react or how it might affect her."

"George, I do understand your predicament but please promise me that you'll keep a record of what I tell you for passing on to Jill and maybe Walter one day."

"Father, I promise you I shall do that."

In early 1953, a telegram arrived for George informing him that his father had passed away; much as George was saddened to receive this news, he knew it was inevitable and in many ways he was just grateful that he had had the time that he had had with his father in recent years. He immediately made arrangements to be at the funeral but was unable to persuade Isabel to join him; ever since the death of Paul, she had become more reclusive and following the death of her father five years after the War ended, had rarely made an appearance in public.

Following her father's death, Isabel and George had moved into his house at Montfiquet; it had been left unoccupied after being vacated by the Germans as Isabel's father could not face the thought of living somewhere where he was convinced numerous atrocities had been masterminded. Instead, he had lived with Isabel and George, thereby allowing him to comfort Isabel following the loss of Paul. By the time George and Isabel moved in, the house was showing signs of neglect but thankfully minimal damage caused by its most recent, unwelcome occupants. George was keen to restore the property to its pre-war condition and for Isabel to be involved in the same way she had been with the hotel in the hope that it would give her something to think about other than the loss of her father and Paul.

With her valued input, it took two years for the work on the home at Montfiquet to be completed. Isabel worked on the interior and George devoted most of his energies to the gardens but, by the end of it, the property was back to its former glory, fit as it once had been for a king and his mistress. Following completion of the work, George was anxious to ensure that Isabel was not left with too much time on her hands and not enough interests to occupy her, fearing she might otherwise withdraw again from public life. With the hotel business still occupying much of his time, George was keen that Isabel too was involved with its business, not least so that he could keep a close eye on her. One proposal he put to her was to work with him on targeting American, British and Canadian guests who could combine a stay at the hotel with a visit to the beaches at which the D-Day landings had taken place. Initially Isabel was not sure how to go about this but each year the number of reservations at the hotel by American guests, in particular during the first fortnight in June, was up on the previous year. To take advantage of these increased bookings, George also offered private tours for those who wanted to hear first-hand what it had been like living in the area during the War, particularly from locals, such as Claude, who could recount their own experiences of the fighting around D-Day. George was concerned that such an initiative might bring back bad memories for Isabel but she threw herself into it and, with her French accent, became a most popular guide with the English-speaking tourists.

By the end of the 1950s, the hotel business was thriving. Bookings were at full capacity for the summer season and the quality of food at the restaurant was not matched by any other restaurant in the region. June, with the organised trips to the nearby beaches, was a particularly busy time and, by the time the summer was over, George and Isabel looked forward to taking things more easily. After the June trips to the beaches were over one year, Isabel noticed that her sleep at night time was disturbed by headaches; at first she thought nothing of it, putting it down to tiredness but by the beginning of August, the headaches were more persistent and were causing her more discomfort. Although painkillers provided some relief, they were not a cure and she knew she had to consult her doctor. The doctor knew what her symptoms might mean, but he was unwilling to tell her his suspicions without a second opinion. He recommended that she consult a neurologist. George persuaded her to consult one in Paris, because the best and most experienced neurologists were based there.

It was another two weeks before Isabel could be seen. Then, being every bit as anxious as Isabel to know what was wrong with her, George travelled with her to Paris. The neurologist conducted various tests, including a cerebral angiography test, which had only recently been developed but which would show the condition of blood vessels in and around the brain. The results of the tests would not be known for at least a week so they returned home in the same state of anxiety.

After two weeks had passed, the neurologist wrote to Isabel telling her the results were known and asking her to arrange another appointment with him so that he could discuss the results with her and George if he was available. After yet another week, George and Isabel arrived at his consulting room fearing the worst; if nothing was wrong, he would have told them by letter or over the phone. Their fears were confirmed. Isabel had a brain tumour and the tumour was at such a stage that it was inoperable. Medical research had reached the stage where some forms of cancer could be treated by chemotherapy, but that was not yet the case with brain tumours. Isabel was unlikely to live for more than another six months.

The neurologist's prognosis proved to be all too true and she passed away just four months after she was first diagnosed with her cancer. During her illness, she never complained and, until she was left with no choice but to resort to morphine to cope with the pain, she acted as if nothing was wrong despite knowing her time would soon be up. George too went about his day-to-day life as if nothing was up, trying to put on a brave face for Isabel. Although he knew it was only a matter of time before Isabel succumbed, it still came as a terrible blow when she died and it dawned on him that the only immediate family he had left were his brother's daughter and her son.

As George adjusted to life alone, he contemplated whether he should move back to England but, on reflection, recognised that, having lived in France for the past forty years, he had lost contact with any friends he had had there. All his friends lived in France. The only exception was Olivia. It crossed his mind to contact her. After all, she had once been the person he had expected to spend the rest of his life with but, after milling the idea over, he chose not to. Hearing from him was more likely to cause Olivia distress than it would any desire to rekindle their relationship.

George's last years were spent alone in France. During that time, he kept the promise he had made to his father to record his family history for passing on to Walter, his father's great-grandson. Knowing that Walter and his mother were George's only relations, he could think of no one better to leave his estate to when he died. With this in mind, he wrote to a firm of lawyers in London, the same firm that had dealt with his father's affairs when his father had passed away, asking if they could draw up a will for him. The person George was corresponding with at the solicitors' firm was a young man called William Haine and, on Haine's advice, George decided to leave all his estate to Walter rather than to Walter's mother, to avoid a second hit of death duties on anything he left to her when she died. Haine recommended that George execute his will in Haine's presence and, as a consequence, George made his final trip to England in 1976 to sign his will. At his meeting with Haine, George explained that it might well be that Walter, the beneficiary of his estate, would not know who George was and, were that to be the case when George died, Haine was to tell Walter that he should speak to his grandmother Olivia to see if she can help. Haine thought better of delving any deeper into the mysteries surrounding the circumstances which had led his client to want to leave his estate to someone he had not met and who did not know him.

Ten years before he made his will, George had sold the hotel business in Bayeux. Much as he enjoyed the company of the guests, he no longer had the same energy to manage it in the way he had when he was younger and rather than allow standards to fall, decided it was time for someone else to take over the running of the hotel. The reputation the hotel had built up under George's management meant that he was able to get a good price for it and more than enough to let him live the rest of his life in comfort. The money he did not need to cover his day-to-day living expenses was entrusted with the stockbroking firm his father had worked for and their shrewd advice enabled George not only to increase the value of his investments but also provide him with healthy dividends.

As his wealth was increasing, his health was deteriorating - his mind was not affected by his aging but his physical condition was. The aches in his joints were causing more pain and he was becoming more and more dependent on painkillers and much as they eased his pain, they disguised the poor condition he was in.

When Madame Dupont, George's housekeeper, arrived for work on the morning of 11th November 1979, she was not surprised that there were no sounds from within the chateau because George was seldom up before she arrived but as the morning wore on without any noise, she started to be concerned about George. Reluctant to disturb him in his bedroom, she went in search of the gardener, Monsieur Dunard and explained her dilemma. Although Monsieur Dunard's and Madame Dupont's paths rarely crossed despite having worked for the same employer for the best part of twenty years, Monsieur Dunard appreciated that it would be inappropriate for Madame Dupont to disturb their master in his private quarters and accepted that it was down to him to do so. Inside the chateau Madame Dupont escorted him to George's bedroom. He knocked on George's bedroom door several times, each knock louder than the previous one but none of them were answered. He had no choice but to open the door and check up on George.

On entering the room, Monsieur Dunard saw George lying on his side in his pyjamas on the bedroom floor, not moving. George's face was pale and he did not respond when Monsieur Dunard called out asking if he was alright. Monsieur Dunard approached George and taking his hand, felt his wrist for the pulse. He could not feel any throbbing. He then opened George's pyjama top to see if he could feel any heartbeat, but to no avail. His final check was to see if he could detect any breathing. Not detecting any breathing he turned to Madame Dupont, who was standing by the bedroom door and told her to call a doctor urgently.

It took less than an hour for a doctor to arrive but less than twenty seconds for the doctor to confirm that George had died. The doctor was able to tell Monsieur Dunard and Madame Dupont that, in his view, the cause of death was in all probability a heart attack.

George was eighty-three years old when he died. By the time of his death, he had fought in and survived one World War and lived through another one. Both though had been at great cost to him and his family. It was perhaps an irony that the day he should die was 11th November, the eighty-first anniversary of the day the First World War came to an end and a date on which its ending is commemorated across much of the world.

Part 8

1980

When Wally finished reading the notebook, he handed it to Flick. Tempted as he was to tell her what he had read, he chose not to. Instead, he thought it would be better for her to read it for herself than for him to summarise it, knowing full well that any summarisation by him would not do it justice.

He did not disturb her as she turned the pages. Judging by the look on her face as she was reading it, he was not sure he could have disturbed her anyway. After taking her almost four hours to read it, Flick closed the notebook and stared at its leather cover without saying a word.

"Well?" enquired Wally, seeing that she had finished. "What d'you make of it?"

"It's almost as if there's too much to take in. I felt I was reading more about a stranger than someone who might have been your grandfather."

"Why d'you say someone who might have been my grandfather? Surely there can't be any doubt he was. What feels a bit strange though is that, until now, it seems that the only person who knows he was my grandfather was my grandmother."

"I didn't mean it like that. I'm sure he was your grandfather but because we hadn't been aware of his existence, it felt as though I was reading about someone else's life."

"Now you know it was my grandfather, what d'you think about what happened to him?"

Flick thought about that for a moment and, instead of answering his question, told Wally that, as it was his grandfather and not hers, she thought he should answer his own question first.

"Wally, as he was your grandfather, I think you should tell me your thoughts about him before I share mine with you."

"OK then. My first impression is that he had a life full of sadness; the First World War cost him the first love of his life and the Second World War cost him the one and only child he knew he had. My second impression is that, despite all the sad events in his life, he was a survivor, surviving not just the sad events but also the numerous threats to his own life during the Wars." Wally then asked Flick what her impressions were.

"Like you, I think it's the sad events in his life that stand out but there were also so many positives in his life and we shouldn't lose sight of them. He had an adventurous life and a charmed one in that he survived when so many of his contemporaries didn't. Even comparing him to his own brother, who d'you think had the more fulfilling life? The brother who may have been fortunate enough to marry the woman your grandfather loved but who was injured in the First World War and killed in the Second or your grandfather who married the second love of his life and survived both Wars intact? I know whose life I'd rather have had."

After spending many hours talking about the life of Wally's grandfather, a life Wally had only just read about, Wally asked Flick whether she thought his grandmother ever discovered his grandfather had not been killed in the First World War.

"Wally, if you remember, when we first mentioned a George Hart to your grandmother, she owned up to knowing him and telling us he was your grandfather; she also told us that he died in the War. I don't think she'd have said that if she thought he'd lived."

Wally thought about this but was not convinced. "Maybe she was being metaphorical when she said he died; maybe she just meant that, as far as she was concerned, he was no longer a part of her life and therefore as good as dead."

"Possibly, but if she knew he hadn't died, she didn't need to hide it from us. Don't forget she did not hide from us the fact that he was your grandfather."

"Or maybe it's just that her memory is such that all she can remember now is being told that he had died in the War and therefore that is genuinely what she believes."

"I suppose that's possible as well but I thought it was more her short-term memory she was losing. If that's the case, surely she would remember being told if he had survived?"

"I suppose so. Or perhaps, feeling guilty about marrying his brother, pretending he was dead was her way of dealing with her guilt."

"That's possible too but again would you say that was a good enough reason for telling us he'd died?"

"Not really. I guess we'll never know for certain unless we ask her and even if we do ask her, we can't be sure she will be telling us the truth or if you can even remember it."

"If you're suggesting we ask her, I don't think we should."

"Why not?"

"If you were to ask her whether or not she knew he had survived the War, don't you think it might make her wonder why you are asking her? Would it not make her think that you're only asking her because you believe or know he survived? And, if she were to think he had survived when she had previously thought this was not the case, how would she feel about that?"

"I don't know; I suppose we shouldn't ask her but that'll mean we'll never know if she knew George survived and we'll never be able to tell her."

"Wally, I think that's right but I really don't think it matters if she knows or not. What's more important is that you know the truth."

Having agreed that they were not going to ask his grandmother if she knew if his grandfather had survived, this left them contemplating whether to tell Wally's mother. Unlike the situation with Wally's grandmother, they were in no doubt that Wally's mother had no idea that her real father was not the man she knew as her father, but his brother instead.

Wally asked Flick how she would react if she was suddenly told that her father was not who she thought he was.

"I'd be shocked at first and maybe wouldn't believe it or at least would not want to believe it. But it would be different for me because my father is still alive, whereas your mother's is not. Still though, I think it would come as a shock to her and something she might find difficult to take in. You have to appreciate that it's different for you knowing George was your mother's father because you never knew his brother, whereas your mother was brought up thinking the brother was her father."

"How do we explain to her then that I'm now the owner of a chateau in France?"

"Good question but, if you remember, before you came here, you told your parents that you were having to spend some time in France managing the finances of a client. You either have to tell them the truth or you have to come up with some plausible explanation as to why you own a chateau in France and, if you decide to live in the chateau, why you're moving to France."

"The fact that I now own the chateau does not mean I'm necessarily moving to France. I could rent it out or sell it. I need more time to decide what I want to do with it and in the meantime, my parents don't need to know I own it or how I came to own it."

"OK, so you can keep that from them but d'you think you should also keep from them the fact that George was your mother's father?"

"You've already told me I shouldn't tell my mother. And, if I was to tell my father, don't you think he would feel he should tell my mother? Is this something a husband should keep from his wife?"

"No, I don't think it is something your father should keep from your mother and I hope that, if we get married, there will be no secrets between us either. If you don't want your mother to know, you shouldn't tell your father."

"Agreed."

"What's agreed? To not telling your father or to there being no secrets between us?"

"Both. That leaves me with one last question to ask about my grandfather, at least for the time being. D'you think he ever knew or suspected that my mother was his child?"

"Nothing in his notebook tells us he knew so we'll never know, but I do think he would have mentioned it if he knew. And, if he ever suspected it, don't you think he would have tried to find out?"

"I suppose so but maybe the thought never crossed his mind. Or maybe he thought it was better not to know and left it at that."

"I guess you're right. So in the same way your mother doesn't know that he was her father, it seems he didn't know she was his daughter and perhaps that was best for both of them. What they didn't know doesn't seem to have done either of them any harm."

And thus it was that Wally discovered the true identity of his grandfather and the true ancestry of his mother, a discovery he chose not to share with his mother.

Over the ensuing months, Wally toyed with the idea of keeping the chateau but in the end decided he was not going to live in France. He put in on the market in the hope of finding a buyer who would appreciate and value living in a home with so much history.

It was not until the following summer that he found such a buyer. But before that, he made up his mind over one other important matter.

Over dinner one evening he asked Flick whether she could remember their conversation about not keeping secrets from each other.

"Of course I do Wally, but why d'you ask?"

"Well, are there any secrets between us?"

"Wally, if you remember exactly what I said, I agreed that there should be no secrets between us but I qualified that by adding there should be no secrets between us if we marry."

"Does that mean, unless we marry, there will be secrets you want to keep from me?"

"No, not necessarily, but you should be able to work out for yourself that there's one way of ensuring I won't keep secrets from you."

"In which case, as I don't want you to keep any secrets from me - will you marry me?"

Flick was tempted to ask Wally if he was only proposing to her because he wanted to know her secrets but thought better of it. And having thought better of it, she did not hesitate to accept Wally's proposal. And even though her parents would have preferred that she was married from their family home, she did not hesitate to agree to Wally's request that they be married in the same church in which his grandfather had married Isabel and that the reception be held in the chateau he had agreed to sell. Neither Wally's parents nor Flick's parents ever understood why Wally and Flick chose to marry in France but their reason for doing so and for holding the reception at a nearby chateau was one secret Wally and Flick knew they would be keeping to themselves.

Part 9

1953

As George approached St Mary's Church in Barnes, he wondered whether he would know or recognise any of the other mourners attending his father's funeral. George realised that, having lived to the age of eighty-five, his father was likely to have out-lived a number of his friends and George knew from the few funerals he had attended before his father's, the longer one lived the fewer were left to attend one's own funeral. One exception to this rule of thumb was where the deceased came from a large family, where the turn-out was usually higher, sometimes if only because some of those attending were keen to find out whether or not they had been remembered in the deceased's will.

George recognised though that this would not apply in the case of his father, whose only surviving family, other than George, consisted of his daughter-in-law Olivia, his granddaughter and his great-grandson, the last of whom would be too young to attend. Wondering whether Olivia would be there, George expected that she would be if only because she was unlikely to have any good reason not to be.

George was not sure how to prepare himself for the possibility of seeing her again. He had last seen her thirty-six years ago and he was by no means certain that he would recognise her after all this time. As for her daughter, he had never met her but she would not be much older than Olivia was when he had last seen her and he was curious to know if the daughter looked like Olivia.

By the time George entered the church, most of those attending were already seated in their pews.

As he slowly made his way to the empty pew at the front on the right hand side of the nave which seemed as though it had been reserved for him, he avoided eye contact with the other mourners. During the service, the vicar gave a short eulogy. It was clear that he knew little about Albert Hart's family or life. George thought it sad that the eulogy had been left to the vicar and that none of those who knew his father best were alive or, if they were alive, none were able and willing to give it. On reflection, he wondered whether he should have been asked but realised that those arranging his father's funeral might not have known of his existence.

Once the service was over, the congregation made its way to the wake which was held in the Barnes Memorial Hall nearby. As he was about to make his way back down the nave to leave the church, George saw two women leave one of the pews on the opposite side of the nave. The first to leave the pew was the younger of the two and although he had never seen her before, he knew by her looks that she was Olivia's daughter. As she was leaving, the younger woman noticed him. George then looked at the second woman. Although her hat covered much of her face, there was no mistaking her. She raised her head and cast her eyes in his direction, fixing her gaze at him. Judging by the look on her face as she looked across, George was in no doubt that Olivia had recognised him.

With Olivia apparently lost for words and not knowing what to say, he broke the silence.

"Hello Olivia."

There was no need to say any more.

Too confused to know how to respond, seeing for the first time a man she had been forced against her will to believe had died over thirty-five years ago, Olivia held her stare for a good five seconds more before looking away and making her way out of the church ahead of George.

Most of those attending the funeral service also attended the wake but George noticed that, whereas her daughter was there, Olivia was not. Wanting to avoid too many questions about how he knew the deceased, George kept to himself as much as he could and was on the point of leaving when he saw Olivia's daughter heading towards him. George knew that she was coming to talk to him and that there was no way he could avoid her without appearing rude.

"Hello, I noticed you in the church. My name is Jill Mortimer. Thank you for coming to my grandfather's funeral. I don't think we have met before so please forgive me if we have. How did you know my late grandfather?"

George hesitated before answering, knowing that he could hardly tell her the truth.

"I was brought up in Barnes and knew the family well when I was a child. Since then though, I have lost touch with the family. So you are Albert's granddaughter; did he have any other relations?"

"I only know of me and my son. There's also my mother who is his daughter-in-law, if you count her. You said you knew the family as a child - did you know my father, Edward?"

"I did indeed but I haven't seen him for over thirty years as I moved to France at the end of the First World War. I heard though that he was killed in the Second World War."

"That's correct; his office in the City was bombed whilst he was at work."

"I'm sorry to hear that." Not wanting to get embroiled in too much conversation with Jill, George explained that he had to be on his way as he had a train to catch back to France that evening, before thanking her for introducing herself to him.

Jill was puzzled why she should be thanked for introducing herself but thought nothing more of it. Little did she know that she was being thanked because meeting her had meant so much to George, even if he could not tell her that they were related to each other.

That evening Jill telephoned her mother to check she had made it home safely after the funeral. During the call, Jill told her mother about her meeting at the wake an old family friend who had known her father.

On being asked by her mother who the old family friend was, Jill replied "I'm not sure. I know I should've asked him his name. He had to leave to catch a train back to France and he'd gone before I realised I hadn't got round to asking him his name."

Olivia knew though that the family friend Jill had met could only have been George, the father Jill never knew she had.

The journey back to France gave George time to reflect. He was convinced Olivia had recognised him even before he spoke to her but he could not even contemplate what she must now be thinking, knowing that he had survived the War. He was pleased that he had met her daughter but not for one moment did it ever cross his mind that she might also be his daughter.

Acknowledgements

Whilst this book is a work of fiction, there are a small number of passages rooted in fact. For example, my grandfather served in the Royal Flying Corps in the First World War and his experiences as a pilot included a German pilot shooting at him with a revolver whilst he was engaged in "patrolling, observation and photography". Had I not been aware that such incidents had taken place, I would have thought them too unbelievable to include them, so I am grateful that they were recorded in a book my father wrote for our family about our family history.

I am also most grateful to Bob Fowke at YouCaxton for his editorial input and advice which the readers will appreciate as much as I do.

About the Author

This is the author's third book and his first novel. He and his wife have four adult children and live in Oxfordshire, but not with their children anymore.

Printed in Great Britain
by Amazon